Tentacle Torment

Blade stared at the Watcher, whose yellow eyes stared back at him. Just as Blade threw himself to one side, a beam of dazzling white light flared from one of the glassy-blue muzzles in the Watcher's head. It played across Blade's sword, and when it passed on, it left the metal blackened and warped.

As Blade sprang to his feet, the Watcher's arms lashed out. The eight-foot steel tentacle whipped around Blade's knees, while the claw on the upper arm unfolded until it could span Blade's waist. He was jerked off his feet and into the air. He tried to swing himself toward the body of the Watcher. If he could get a firm grip and then start hacking at the Watcher's joints with the knife from his belt . . .

Blade never made it. The head turned toward him, and Blade had a moment of staring in the mouth of one of the blue tubes—a moment just long enough for him to know that he was about to die. . . .

THE BLADE SERIES:

BLADE

CITY OF THE LIVING DEAD
by Jeffrey Lord

PINNACLE BOOKS   LOS ANGELES

BLADE #26: CITY OF THE LIVING DEAD

Copyright © 1978 by Lyle Kenyon Engel

An original Pinnacle Books edition, published for the first time anywhere.

Produced by Lyle Kenyon Engel, Book Creations, Inc., Canaan, N.Y. 12029

ISBN: 0-523-40193-0

First printing, March 1978

Cover illustration by Carl Lundgren

Printed in the United States of America

PINNACLE BOOKS, INC.
One Century Plaza
2029 Century Park East
Los Angeles, California 90067

CITY OF THE LIVING DEAD

Chapter 1

Richard Blade sat down in the chair in the glass booth far below the Tower of London. He felt the rubber of the chair's back and seat cold against his naked, grease-smeared body. He tried to relax while Lord Leighton scurried about, fastening cobra-headed metal electrodes to every part of Blade's skin. Twenty, fifty, a hundred of them. Each one was connected to a wire, and each wire led off into some part of the vast computer that filled the whole rock-walled room. The gray crackle-finished consoles towered above Blade, pressing their tops against the ceiling. Blade always thought it would have seemed more appropriate if the computer had been the master here and the men its servants, instead of the other way around.

Lord Leighton was the master nonetheless, the man who had created the computer out of his own genius and many millions of pounds sterling. In a few more minutes he would use it to send Richard Blade hurtling off into Dimension X. Dimension X was a previously unknown realm of existence discovered by a lucky accident and now being systematically explored by Richard Blade—and Richard Blade alone. There was no other living human being in the world who could travel into Dimension X and return alive and sane.

Lord Leighton finished his work and gave Blade a final inspection. Then he stepped over to the main console for the whole computer and stood within easy reach of the red master switch. Blade followed the white-coated figure with his eyes, about the only part of his own body that he could still comfortably move. Lord Leighton's movements were as brisk as ever—astonishingly brisk for a man past eighty with his spine bent by a hunchback and his legs twisted since childhood by polio. But then Lord Leighton had always ignored the limitations of his body, just as he'd always ignored the wishes and preferences of other people. Neither his own frailties nor the opposition of others had ever been allowed to stand between him and what he wanted to achieve.

Blade looked to one side of the console. The spectator's chair was still folded up into its niche in the wall. It didn't look as though J were going to make it down here in time. A pity, and J would regret it, but it couldn't be helped. The old man had always been busy when he was head of MI6 and Richard Blade was one of his crack agents. He was still busy, now that he worked with Project Dimension X. Things were always unexpectedly coming up to drag him away or chain him to his desk.

Blade turned his attention back to Lord Leighton in the exact moment the scientist's hand gripped the master switch. In a single, smooth motion, he drew it down to the bottom of the slot. Lights danced across the control panel in a continuous ripple of color, and pain swallowed up Richard Blade.

He'd felt pain before—wounds, torture, the pain that exploded and thundered in his head when it was time for him to return to England from Dimension X. Pain was never a friend and could never be one, but it was an old, familiar enemy. At least it had been familiar until now.

This pain was different. This was pain that gripped every part of his body from his scalp to his toes in white-hot pincers, rending and clawing, stripping away the flesh from the bones and tearing one bone from another. The pain blinded him, searing his eyes like molten metal. He couldn't look at himself, but he knew that if he did he would see flesh blistering and blackening and his blood boiling away before it could flow, his exposed bones cracking, his fingers and toes curling up like dead leaves and dropping to the floor. Lord Leighton would be staring in horror, torn out of his scientific detachment. Something had finally and fatally gone wrong. The computer wasn't sending Blade into Dimension X. It was slowly and agonizingly killing him.

Then the computer hurled Blade down into blackness, and as he plunged, Blade felt his body shredding apart, until all

2

that was left was a dimly conscious mind hurtling down through darkness. Then the last dim consciousness vanished, and there was only blackness.

Blade drifted slowly back up to consciousness. He felt a yielding surface under him, then something over him slightly restricting his movements. Some unknown time later he realized he was lying on a bed with a sheet and blankets over him. Suddenly he knew that he was lying safely in his own bed in the bedroom of his own West End flat. His pajamas, the pillow under his head, and the sheet under him were all soaked with sweat.

The nightmare of blazing pain had been just that—a nightmare. He looked at his watch. He would really be on his way to Dimension X in another twelve hours. For the moment he was safely at home, in no danger of anything except falling out of bed. The underground room, Lord Leighton, the computer, the electrodes, the pain—they'd all been creations of his sleeping mind.

Blade suddenly found that he was incredibly thirsty. He threw back the covers and climbed out of bed. He was relieved to discover that he was steady on his feet. He wouldn't expect a nightmare to affect his coordination, but it wasn't impossible. Since he'd entered Project Dimension X, *impossible* was a word Richard Blade refused to use.

Twenty-five times he'd sat down in the chair and been wired into the computer. Twenty-five times Lord Leighton had pulled a switch. Every one of those times the computer had twisted his brain so that all his senses now registered some part of that vast unknown called Dimension X.

The first time it had happened by accident. All the other times it had been deliberate. There was an incredible wealth of knowledge and resources lying out there in Dimension X. If that wealth could be tapped for Britain's use and the secret of Dimension X kept in the meantime—well, all the wealth from the North Sea oil fields would look pitifully small by comparison.

If that wealth could be tapped, if the secret were kept, and *if Richard Blade remained alive and sane long enough.*

How long would be long enough? Nobody knew. So far

there was nobody else alive who could make the round trip. The search for such a person was still going on, but no one expected quick results.

Fortunately, Richard Blade was one of the most perfect specimens of physical and mental development alive. He was very likely the most unkillable human being in the world. He'd faced wild animals and still wilder peoples, both savage and civilized. He'd faced wind and waves, icy cold and searing heat, a dozen kinds of monsters, even an intelligent race of aliens from somewhere far out in interstellar space. He'd survived them all. He was quite prepared to go on pitting himself against the perils of Dimension X as long as he was needed.

Yet—what if his own brain were beginning to turn traitor? Blade knew perfectly well that no human brain was really adapted to being twisted completely around twenty-five successive times. Not even his. The Project had given him psychological problems before—a prolonged period of impotence, a shorter period of excessive drinking. Was this nightmare the first sign of some new problem?

Blade didn't know. He would mention it to Lord Leighton and J, of course. They would pass it on to the Project's staff of psychologists. Meanwhile Blade would be off to Dimension X. One nightmare, however gruesome, wasn't enough reason for cancelling a trip. A gamble? Yes, but every trip into Dimension X was a gamble that would have given a normal person not just one nightmare but fifty.

Richard Blade wasn't quite normal. He was too fond of matching his own skills against great danger to be a very comfortable citizen for any peaceful twentieth-century country. Field intelligence work had been the most rewarding career he could find—until Project Dimension X came along.

At times Blade grumbled over Lord Leighton's latest whims and fancies. At times he felt like a beast of burden. He was never happy over the innocent people who got caught up in his battles and adventures to end up dead or mindless. Yet he could never imagine leaving the Project entirely. It was too important to Britain—and too important to Richard Blade.

4

Blade went to the kitchen, poured himself a tall glass of beer, drank it, and went back to bed. It was several more hours to dawn, and the best thing to do with those hours was sleep. His first few days in a new Dimension were usually rather busy, and it helped to be as well-rested as possible.

Blade's alarm woke him at eight-thirty. The housekeeper appeared and produced the large breakfast that Blade always ate before a trip into Dimension X. Like sleep, food was sometimes rather hard to come by at first in a new Dimension.

Filled with porridge, bacon, eggs, toast, marmalade, and coffee, Blade left the flat and hailed a taxi. The taxi carried him through the traffic-clogged streets of London to the Tower and left him there. The Special Branch men guarding the entrance to the underground complex checked his identification and passed him through. The elevator took him two hundred feet down in a few seconds, and when the door whispered open at the botom, J was waiting for him. Blade couldn't help blinking. The memory of the nightmare was so vivid he'd half expected J not to be on hand for today's departure.

They shook hands. "You look rather surprised to see me, Richard," said the older man. J was nearer seventy than sixty, but the gray eyes in the long aristocratic face missed very little. They never had, one reason why J was still alive.

Blade explained the nightmare as they walked down the long central corridor toward the computer rooms at the other end of the complex. J listened without comment, his face expressionless.

"You think there's no risk to you in going ahead?" he asked, after Blade finished.

"I can't be certain, of course, but I doubt it very much. One nightmare, after all . . ." he shrugged.

"I hope you're right," said J. His face was no longer so expressionless. Blade knew that J loved him like a son and was always troubled at the thought of him running unnecessary risks.

They approached the door to the computer rooms. The last of the electronic monitors scanned them, identified them, and opened the door for them. They passed in through a series of rooms packed with auxiliary equipment and the small army of technicians needed to run it and reached the door to the room holding the main computer. The door slid open, and Lord Leighton ushered them into his private sanctum.

The scientist looked exactly as he had in the nightmare, exactly as he had since Blade first knew him. His lean, twisted frame was enveloped in a ragged laboratory coat that might have been white once, after its last cleaning years ago. His white hair stuck out in the same disorder as always, and his bushy eyebrows seemed as ready to drop like a curtain over the dark, intensely bright eyes.

Blade let J describe the nightmare, while he himself went off to the changing room carved out of the rock wall. At this point in the proceedings, he always disliked waiting one second longer than absolutely necessary.

A few minutes later he stepped out of the changing room, naked except for a loincloth, smeared from head to foot with the black grease that was supposed to prevent electrical burns. It or *something* had always worked. He hadn't been burned yet—except in his nightmare.

Lord Leighton and J had apparently finished their discussion of the nightmare. Lord Leighton seemed to accept that there was nothing to worry about, or else he was simply in one of his untalkative moods.

Blade walked to the center of the room and sat down in the chair inside the glass booth. From then on events marched swiftly, following exactly the same path they'd followed twenty-five times before in real life and once in the nightmare. The only difference between today's reality and last night's ghastly dream was J's presence. Blade sincerely hoped there would be other differences!

In spite of what his reason told him, Blade was tense by the time Leighton stepped up to the control panel. He forced himself to breathe deeply and not stiffen as Leighton's hand came down on the master switch. Then the switch slid down its slot and reached the bottom.

A terrible shrieking and roaring filled the room, like a hundred factory whistles all sounding together. The sound tore at Blade's ears, but there was no pain. An immense wave of relief washed over him, relief that there was no pain, relief that his nightmare was not becoming reality.

Then the floor of the chamber cracked open, and a darkness like liquid tar flowed up around the feet of Blade's chair. He saw it reach his ankles, his knees, his waist, but he felt nothing. He sat motionless, taking deep breaths to fill his lungs, as the liquid darkness rose to the level of his chest. He took a final breath and held it as the darkness rose up to his chin. It rose to cover mouth and nose. He closed his eyes and felt a faint tickling on his eyelids as the darkness rose up over him. It was like being brushed with tiny feathers.

He sat motionless, holding his breath until his chest began to hurt as if white-hot bands of iron were tightening around it. He held his breath for a moment longer, until both head and chest seemed about to disintegrate into hot dust.

Then he breathed in. The blackness that was outside flooded in, and as it flooded in, it drowned all his senses at once.

Chapter 2

Blade awoke with a more than usually violent pain in his head and the feeling of something hard under it. He ignored the hardness and lay still. His head always hurt after he'd passed into Dimension X, and there was never anything to do about it, but wait until it stopped hurting.

Blade kept his eyes closed, breathed regularly, and gradually felt the pain fade from a pounding agony to a dull, distant ache. At that point he opened his eyes and sat up.

All around him was a dull, gray twilight. He was resting in the lee of a house-sized boulder, dark blue with layers of red in it. Around him were strewn a number of other rocks that looked like quartz.

Straight ahead the ground rolled gently away into the distance, covered with waist-high bushes that bore only a few tufts of brown, spikey leaves. Far away a sharp ridge cut off the horizon. Blade rose and headed toward the ridge. It was the only break in the whole dreary landscape around him.

It turned into a race between Blade's march toward the ridge and the coming of darkness. There was barely enough light to see by when he finally reached the top. Below him the ground plunged away into a tortured, rugged slope of bare rock dotted here and there with stunted shrubs. The slope dropped nearly a thousand feet to a level floor of more bare rock. Far off in the gathering darkness rose the other wall of the valley.

A patch of silver-white among the rocks halfway down the slope at his feet caught Blade's eye. He looked more carefully and saw a thin line of silver winding down the slope below the patch. He scrambled down the slope toward it as fast as he dared.

In spite of his care, he twice fell hard enough to get bruised. Several times rocks came loose under his feet and rolled off down the side of the valley, crashing and banging like small cannon. Blade ignored everything, until at last he slide down a near-vertical pitch eight feet high and landed on hands and knees beside the spring.

It gushed from the rock as if it were coming from a fire hose, forced up and out by the pressure underground. It made a twenty-foot arc in the air and splashed down hard enough to throw up the cloud of spray that Blade had seen first. Over the centuries the spring had worn a pool for itself in the rock where it fell. Blade crawled over to the pool and began scooping the water into his mouth. It was lukewarm and tasted faintly of minerals, but it was drinkable.

By now it was completely dark. Blade realized he might be wise to find some place where he'd be invisible both from the ridge and from the floor of the valley. On the other hand, that would mean roaming about among the tangled and treacherous rocks of the valley wall in the darkness. He'd probably be safer staying where he was.

Blade found a flat spot only a few yards from the pool and lay down. The rock was not a particularly soft bed, and he suspected that he'd have a whole crop of fresh bruises in the morning. That hardly mattered. He'd found water, and the weather seemed tolerable.

For the moment that was quite enough—much more than he'd started with in some Dimensions, in fact. He could seek out what else this Dimension held when there was light to see it.

Blade awoke in a chilly dawn to feel a breeze on his bare skin. He stood up and went through a series of brisk exercises to restore his circulation and get any cramps or kinks out of his muscles. When he'd finished, he felt about as ready to face a day's traveling as he could, considering that he still had no clothes, footgear, food, or weapons.

He was bending down to drink when he heard a distant noise that was neither the wind, the water, nor rocks rolling down the valley wall. He straightened up and listened. With tantalizing slowness, the sound grew louder and took on recognizable forms. Blade heard the blare of trumpets and the thud of slowly beaten drums echoing among the rocks. Then he heard the sound of many feet moving steadily.

Blade scrambled down the slope toward the valley floor, keeping low and looking for a place where he could see without being seen. He found it—a shallow depression in the ground, screened from the side by two large boulders. He dropped flat and stared downslope just as the approaching men emerged out of the mist eddying across the valley floor.

It was quite a procession—three hundred men at least, with two hundred animals and more than thirty wagons, carts, and litters. As he got a better look at the party, Blade realized he'd better be particularly on the alert. If this weren't a military expedition, he'd like to know what else to call it.

Ahead, behind, and on either flank rode forty men mounted on almost comically misshapen beasts. They looked as though someone had started to draw a horse but got so drunk while doing it that the rear end came out very different from the front.

The head could have belonged to a horse, except for the enormous protruding ears. The forelegs were double-jointed and ended in three sharp-clawed toes, and the body was thinner than any horse could ever be without starving to death. The hind legs looked as if they might have been borrowed from a kangaroo, long, heavy-boned, and immensely muscular, with sharp, jutting spurs. The creature trailed off into six feet of flattened tail, ending in a mass of bone. Blade noticed that the tails were strapped tightly in place. Doubtless they were unstrapped in battle, so the beasts could use them as weapons.

The creatures were dark green with irregular patterns of grayish-brown stripes, except for white tails and ears. They might look ludicrous, but Blade suspected they would be unpleasantly formidable opponents in battle.

The riders wore chain mail shirts over broad-skirted leather coats and plate leg armor over blue leather trousers. They wore high-crested helmets with jointed cheekpieces, and all were bearded. All of them had a shield and a light ten-foot lance, and either two swords or a sword and a vicious-looking double-bladed axe with a four-foot handle. The weapons and armor looked well worn, and the men themselves were tanned, scarred, and relaxed in their saddles. They had the stamp of veterans all over them.

So did the men marching on foot. There were about a hundred of them, in two lines. They were dressed like the cavalry, except for the leg armor. All of them carried sword and shield. About half carried bows and quivers, while the other half carried long matchlock muskets and powder horns.

Between the two lines of infantry was a mixed column of men, beasts, and vehicles. There were five small cannon on crude mountings, no more than blocks of wood with wheels attached. There were a score of ox-carts, some piled high with canvas-covered sacks and chests, others rattling along empty. There was a pair of four-wheeled wagons covered with embroidered red curtains. Blade heard female voices and laughter coming from behind the curtains. There were two more low-slung wagons, each carrying four barred wooden cages. Blade heard a hissing sound as the two wagonloads of cages rattled past and thought he smelled a faint animal musk.

In the middle of everything was a palanquin curtained with gilded leather and decorated with floral designs in silver picked out with jewels. In front a pole supported a long banner, pale green, showing a black claw holding a burning torch. Eight heavily muscles bearers carried the palanquin. Except for shoulder pads, loinclothes, boots, and ankle chains, they were naked. Two more eight-man bearer teams marched behind the palanquin, under the guard of a dozen soldiers wearing blue-lacquered helmets and silvered mail.

A punitive expedition, a royal progress, a general's tour of inspection, a tax-gatherer's visit, or what?

There were enough men and animals and gear for the party to be any of these things, or several of them at once. He decided to follow them for a while, although he'd keep his distance at first. He didn't want to find out the hard way that these people killed or enslaved strangers on sight.

Whatever the men were and wherever they were going, they were going there fast. The drums thudded, the trumpets blared, wheels banged and rumbled over rock, ungreased axles squealed, hooves and feet clattered and thumped. In a few minutes the whole party was past, and the last rider was disappearing in the mist. Blade waited until the noise started to fade away, then scrambled down to the valley floor and set out in pursuit.

The trail showed poorly on the hard rock, but the soldiers made so much noise that only a deaf man could have had any trouble following them. Blade kept a good mile behind them, out of sight in the mist, stopping whenever silence from ahead told him the soldiers had stopped. Twice he dropped back even farther as the mist lifted briefly. Otherwise he was on the move all day, his long legs easily keeping pace with the soldiers ahead.

The soldiers kept on through the thickening mist of evening until the light was gone. Then they made camp. From the splashing sounds, Blade guessed they'd made camp around a stream or spring. Wearily, he resigned himself to a chill and thirsty night. He decided he'd scout out the camp, though, just to see what more he could learn about these people.

He made his approach two hours after dark and promptly learned one thing. The soldiers had made a circle of their wagons and crept inside that circle like mice into their holes. They hadn't even bothered to post a guard over the spring. Blade took advantage of that, drinking the ice-cold water until his thirst was gone. Then he made a complete circle around the camp, coming so close that he felt he could almost reach out through the mist and touch the wagons. Except for the occasional lowing of the draft animals or the choking snore of a restless soldier, the camp was as silent as the rest of the dark valley.

Blade refused to believe this was sheer carelessness. These men looked like experienced soldiers who wouldn't leave a camp unguarded without some good reason. Either they knew there was nothing prowling the valley by night that could do them any harm, or there was something against which there was no possible defense. That was not a pleasant thought, and Blade found himself looking cautiously around him and taking extra care to move silently.

13

Then he laughed softly to himself. If the soldiers who knew this land had decided there was no point in losing sleep, he would take his cue from them. He retreated to a safe distance and found level ground behind a large boulder that would conceal him when dawn came. Then he settled down for another night of trying to find soft spots in the rocks.

Chapter 3

The camp woke at dawn with a burst of human and animal voices, drums and trumpets, and the clatter of equipment and weapons. Blade listened, trying to make out what was being said.

He knew that if he made out any words he'd be able to understand them. As he passed into each new Dimension, the computer somehow altered his brain so that the language of that Dimension came to him as plain English—and his own speech came out in the new language. He'd experienced this miracle every time he went into Dimension X, but even Lord Leighton and the Project's best neurologists didn't understand exactly how the miracle took place.

Unfortunately, he was too far off to make out any words. He started crawling closer, but before he'd covered half the distance, the soldiers were marching off again. All he could make out was, "Hud, na, na, ni! Hud, na, na, ni!"—which was probably nothing more than a marching cadence and certainly didn't tell him very much. He settled down to another day on the trail of the soldiers.

After about three hours, the ground began to slope sharply upward. The mist began to thin out, until Blade could look ahead and see two sharp peaks with a pass between them. The soldiers were climbing a slope that rose up to the pass. Some of the cavalry were already riding back and forth across the pass. Blade found cover and waited, listening to the distant cracking of whips and the lowing of the oxen as they were prodded up the slope. When the last rider had vanished around the flank of the peak to the left, Blade left cover and plunged forward. He saw that the pass was unguarded and went up the slope like a long-distance runner.

Ahead of him a gently rolling, sparsely wooded plain stretched away toward a distant line of hills. High overhead he saw a flock of birds, black specks wheeling against a clear sky. Far away across the plain, he could see the flickering banner and the glint of sunlight on armor and weapons. On the softer ground here, the trail was clearly visible—a wide strip of footprints, hoofmarks, and wheel ruts. The ground was still rock-strewn, but now it was almost covered with coarse grass. With no mist to conceal him, Blade had to drop back until he could barely see the soldiers. At that distance he was quite sure they could hardly make out a lone figure stalking along behind them, even if they were keeping a good watch.

Over the next two hours the ground slowly became more and more overgrown with large bushes and small trees. Blade found he was able to slowly close up on the solders with no risk of being seen. He was within three hundred yards of the rear of the party when a village appeared ahead.

The village seemed large and prosperous. Around it stretched pastures, grain fields, orchards, kitchen gardens, and even a vineyard. The village itself was completely surrounded by a stone wall crowned with thorny branches. The buildings inside were either sod or stone, and all had heavily thatched roofs. The smoke from many hearths and fires rose from brick chimneys.

As the soldiers marched past, the farmers working in the fields or pruning the trees threw them brief glances. Then they went back to work, as if the soldiers were no more interesting than a light shower of rain and somewhat less important than an escaped pig.

The closer the soldiers got to the village, the more alert they seemed. The mounted men were trying to look in all directions at once, and the infantry marched with their heads up and their hands on their swords. Blade saw men climbing down from the wagons and walking close behind the five cannon.

The soldiers marched out on to a broad area of flat, beaten earth directly in front of the gate of the village. The drums beat a long roll, and the trumpets blasted out an even longer, ear-torturing peal that seemed to go on forever. Blade listened from behind a wall in the orchard, less than a hundred yards away. He half expected the village wall to collapse from the sheer volume of noise, like the walls of Jericho and Joshua's trumpets.

The noise—it could hardly be called music—died away. By now the infantry was drawn up in two lines, the musketeers in front and the archers in back. The wagons stood behind the infantry, and the cannon rested on either flank. Gunners stood behind each of the cannon, lighted matches in their hands. The cavalry was riding around the village at a slow trot, their shields on their arms and their lances held ready for action.

The curtains of the palanquin opened, and its occupant climbed out. Blade could see that he was more than six feet tall and wore a blue robe with a white sash. He carried a golden helmet under one arm and had a long curved sword slung across his back. He put on the helmet and appeared to be closely examining the village. The gate was still tightly closed. The man drew his sword, waved it at the wall, and shouted loudly:

"In the name of the Shoba, as Aygoon of the Tribute, I call the village of Hores to the business of the day."

There was no response. The Aygoon repeated the summons, shouting louder and waving the sword more vigorously. Still silence. He did everything a third time, and this time he looked to Blade as if he were about to have a fit.

Without a word the Aygoon waved his sword at one of the cannon. The gunner thrust his match into the touchhole, and the gun went off with a *whooomp* and a thick cloud of white smoke. Dust and stone chips flew from the village wall where the shot struck. The Aygoon waited for the dust to clear, then waved his sword at another cannon.

Whooomp! Whooomp! Whooomp! Three cannon went off in rapid succession, and all three balls struck the same section of wall as the first one. The wall shivered, and a six-foot section of the crest went down with a crash and a rumble. A final shot from the last gun smashed one of the hinges of the gate.

Blade heard angry shouts from inside the wall, but the gate remained closed. Some of the archers stepped forward and sent arrows arching over the wall into the village. This drew more shouts and a few screams. The archers kept up a low but steady fire until the cannon were reloaded.

Now the gunners unfastened the rear wheels from one of the cannon so that the breech end of the carriage dropped to the ground. The gunner pressed the match down into the touchhole, and the gun hurled a shot clear over the wall to land among the houses. Blade heard even louder screams, this time of pain, and the unmistakable crashing and crackling of a roof caving in.

That ended the defiance of the villagers. Perhaps they'd hoped their stubbornness would make the soldiers hesitate or even withdraw. Perhaps they'd just been bluffing. In any case, the soldiers hadn't hesitated, the bluff had been called, and the cannon were ready to hammer the village into rubble about the ears of its people.

The screams and shouts from the village died away. Then the gate opened, and the people began filing out to face the Shoba's soldiers. Someone in the village began pounding away on a gong. Blade saw the farmers and herdsmen in the fields and pastures drop their tools and staffs and begin running toward the village. Some of them had stripped to loincloths and came in such a hurry that they didn't even bother to dress.

The people of the village might not be willing to face destruction, but they still weren't willing to crawl to their enemies. They came out with their heads up and their faces blank. A few children burst into tears at the sight of the soldiers drawn up before them, but were quickly hushed by their mothers.

At last the whole village was assembled, ready to submit to the Shoba's demands. Blade counted nearly a thousand people, including more than two hundred men of military age.

Now the blue-robed Aygoon stepped forward, and from the ranks of the villagers, their chief stepped forward to meet his enemy. Blade had no trouble recognizing the chief for what he was. He wore only soiled white breeches and san-

18

dals, and his only sign of rank was a wide copper band around his left arm just above the elbow. Yet the villagers stepped aside to make a path for him, and although he was a small man, he carried himself so that he seemed eight feet tall. The Shoba might take anything else from his people, but not their pride.

The discussion between the chief and the Aygoon was short, and Blade couldn't hear a word of it. Then the soldiers went into action. They plunged into the ranks of the villagers and one by one hauled out twelve young men. These were promptly dragged off behind the wagons and chained together.

Then the Aygoon clapped his hands together and shouted a single word. A ripple went through the villagers, and the soldiers promptly raised their muskets and arrows. The tension-filled silence lasted another moment; then the chief slowly nodded. Twenty men turned silently and walked back through the gate.

They were back out in a few minutes. Eighteen of them staggered under the weight of bulging sacks of grain. Two carried wooden trays covered with white cloths. On each tray was stacked a pile of small metal bars. Even from a hundred yards away, Blade could not mistake the sheen of pure gold.

The men laid the sacks and the gold at the feet of the Aygoon and stepped back. The Aygoon tapped each bag and the two stacks of gold with his sword, nodded, and started to turn away. Blade could almost feel the tension go out of the air. In spite of the ominous beginning, the day's business was ending peacefully. The Shoba's men weren't the type to provoke a fight purely for their own amusement—just about what Blade would have expected if they were as well-trained as they seemed to be.

Then, in a single moment, the peace came in an end. A small head appeared over the top of the wall in the middle of the section battered by the cannon. The child seemed to recognize somebody among the twelve young men now shackled to the wagons and let out a shrill scream. The Aygoon shouted and dropped into a fighting stance, sword raised in both hands. Then he shouted again, and half a dozen of the musketeers raised their weapons and let fly. Their mus-

19

kets weren't particularly accurate, but there were enough of them and the range was short. The child's head turned into red paste and dropped out of sight.

A rumble of anger went through the crowd of villagers, punctuated with shrill cries. The rest of the musketeers leveled their pieces, and the archers drew. The chief turned and gestured frantically to his people. Apparently the child's appearance on the wall was a serious breach of one of the Shoba's rules for the tribute-collection days. Only by keeping totally calm could the villagers prevent a massacre.

The angry rumble died into silence. The Aygoon shifted his sword to one hand and seemed to be looking over the people in front of him. Then his free hand shot out, pointing. Again soldiers tramped forward and plunged into the crowd. There was a flurry of movement as they seized someone; then they were coming out into the open again.

They were half carrying, half dragging a slender, dark-haired young woman in a leather skirt and tunic. She cried out as they ripped off the tunic, leaving her bare to the waist.

At the sight of the woman, the village chief quivered all over, as if he'd been struck with a whip. At her cry, he let out a cry of his own, with agony in it as if he'd been stabbed.

"Twana! No!"

The Aygoon said nothing. He merely pointed at the chief. Two of the musketeers came at him, their weapons held high, butt down. The butts swung, and the chief sprawled on the ground, clutching one arm. One of the soldiers kicked him in the groin, and this time there were no words in his scream of agony.

Blade held his breath. He was certain that in the next moment he'd see a bloody massacre as the villagers stormed forward and the soldiers let fly with muskets and bows. Without the iron determination of their chief, what would hold back the villagers?

In that moment Blade would have given an arm and a leg for some weapon that could reach across the distance between him and the Aygoon to strike the man down.

There was no massacre. The musketeers and the archers kept their weapons raised. The cavalry assembled on either side of the villagers, set to ride into the crowd with lances out. The Aygoon stood in the middle of it all, his sword raised, not sparing a look for the man on the ground or the woman his soldiers were now loading into one of the red-curtained wagons. Gradually the villagers' anger and will to fight faded away. Still more gradually they drifted back through the gate into the villager or back out toward their fields and pastures.

Blade didn't wait for the soldiers to form up and march off. He crept away from the wall, then ran through the orchard to the fields. He worked his through the waist-high standing grain until he came to where he'd seen some of the men at work. As he'd guessed, there were clothes and footgear lying scattered where the men had left them. Just as important, there were tools that could be used as weapons. Blade rapidly snatched up a pair of baggy leggings and a goatskin jacket, then a sickle and a six-foot staff of limber, dark wood. He was on his way back into the orchard before the first villagers entered the field. With luck, they'd assume the Shoba's men had carried off the missing articles along with everything else they'd taken and not bother looking for a thief.

No doubt there were Dimensions where people who behaved like the Shoba's soldiers were really the side Blade ought to be on. Perhaps this was one of them. Common sense told Blade that he should wait a little longer before making an enemy of the Shoba. No doubt making an enemy of the Shoba would make him a friend of the villagers, but was it worth it?

It was. Never mind what common sense told him. Blade had to listen to his instincts. Those instincts told him to strike. They told him that people who kidnapped young men and women, who shot small children and smashed up village walls, who carried off gold and grain, were people who would be his enemies sooner or later.

So why not now?

Chapter 4

The Shoba's men marched only about five miles to the south before making camp for the night. They settled in by a thick stand of scrubby trees and sent out woodcutting parties. By the time darkness fell, a score of fires was blazing cheerfully.

From the shelter of the trees, Blade watched the camp settle down. He smelled wood smoke and roasting meat, heard the drunken laughter of soldiers and ragged trumpet-calls. He saw the women's wagons parked in the very center of the camp, but none of the women. Finally, he saw sentries take up positions all around the camp as the fires began to die down.

When Blade saw that, he suspected he wouldn't be able to rescue Twana tonight. He was certain that he could enter the camp and bring her out with surprise on his side. With thirty sentries on the prowl, it would be hard to get that surprise.

Besides, if he struck this close to the village, the Aygoon would probably conclude that the people of Hores were responsible for the incident. Blade and Twana might escape, but not the villagers. The cannon and the soldiers would take a gruesome vengeance on them for what they hadn't done.

Blade wouldn't risk that. He'd wait for a day or two, then move in. By then the soldiers would be a good many miles from Hores, and they'd be less alert. The only other alternative seemed to be doing nothing, and Blade refused to consider that.

The smell of roasting meat from the camp reminded him that he hadn't eaten for two days. He made a brief search of the forest for something edible, found nothing, and resigned himself to sleeping on an empty stomach. The ground under

23

the trees was covered with needles and dead leaves. Compared to sleeping on the bare rock, tonight would be like sleeping on a feather mattress.

Blade found a hiding place well inside the trees, lay down, stretched out, and was comfortably asleep within minutes.

The next morning the soldiers were slow to waken and slow to get on the march. After that, they moved briskly enough and by noon were coming up to a pair of smaller villages. From these they took five men, two dozen goats, and several baskets of fruit. By now it was obvious to Blade that much of the tax or tribute was intended to feed the tax collectors and their animals on the march. The young men and the gold were another matter. The men no doubt went to the Shoba's army and the gold to the treasury.

That night the soldiers camped ten miles beyond the village and five miles from the nearest forest. From behind a low rise in the ground, Blade watched them closely. They built no fires, and only a handful of men came out on sentry duty. The wagons formed a ragged circle more than a hundred yards across, wide open to someone who could move in quickly and silently.

Far off to the southwest, the hills seemed to rise higher than usual. Blade studied them in the dying glow of the sunset and noticed a peculiar *regularity* in their crests. It looked almost as if someone had built a wall along the crest of the whole range. The "wall" seemed to stretch for at least twenty miles before vanishing in the distance. Blade's curiosity was aroused. He found himself hoping that the next day's march would lead him off toward the hills.

Just before dawn Blade woke to hear something scampering past him. He watched several gopher-like creatures pop out of holes in the ground while he quietly picked up his staff in one hand and a loose stone in the other.

Crack, whack, bang. Blade killed three of the creatures before they could get back into their holes, two with the staff and one with a thrown stone. Then he skinned them with the sickle blade and ate them raw. The flesh was gamy, but it was food, and food meant the energy he would badly need.

He saved the skins, which might be useful to protect Twana's feet.

By the time Blade finished his bloody breakfast, the soldiers were moving out again. He was happy to see them swinging off toward the southwest and moved out on their trail the moment it was safe.

By noon Blade could see that the hills ahead rose more than a thousand feet from the plain, their bare flanks always sloping at a forty to sixty-degree angle. Along the crest of the hills ran what was undeniably an artificial structure, a blue-gray wall nearly fifty feet high. It did not run completely level but instead rose and fell slightly with the line of the crest. It reminded Blade very much of pictures he'd seen of the Great Wall of China. Like the Great Wall, it seemed to go on forever.

As the wall came closer, Blade's impression of it began to change. For one thing, it seemed to be made of some solid and homogeneous material rather than built up of individual blocks. The amount of material in just the part of the wall Blade could see must be enough to build a fair-sized city.

There were no towers, there were no gates, there were no stairs or ladders. In many places vines and trees seemed to have sprouted from the hilltops and crept up the wall. Otherwise the outer face of the wall was as bare and unbroken as the face of a dam.

At times Blade thought he saw a faint gold-tinged shimmering along the top of the wall, like waves of heat in the air over a hot road. Twice he thought he saw the sunlight reflected from a large surface of brightly polished metal. Once he could have sworn the metal surface was *moving* along the top of the wall, at least when he first saw it. When he looked again, it had stopped. When he looked a third time, it had vanished.

The mystery of the wall grew each time Blade looked at it. Certainly it would be the next thing he'd study in this Dimension, after he'd rescued Twana and returned her to Hores.

Or he might have to study the wall even before that. If he and Twana didn't get clean away, the wall offered a possible escape route. If the trees and vines grew on one side of the wall to provide a way up, they probably grew on the other side to provide a way down. The soldiers might be able to climb up after him, but they could hardly get their mounts over the wall. Blade was quite certain he could keep ahead of them on foot.

First, however, he had to get Twana free. There seemed to be no more villages in sight, and by now it was midafternoon. The soldiers might be making a rather ragged camp tonight. That would give Blade an opportunity to strike—as good a one as he could expect.

The darkness reduced everything to ghost shapes. Deep inside the camp, Blade saw two torches glowing faintly among the wagons. Each torch threw a faint circle of pale yellow light. Everywhere else there was blackness and starlight. Sometimes an ox or riding animal would stamp or rattle its harness. Otherwise all was silent. The whole camp might have been dead, not just asleep.

Three hundred yards from the camp, Blade went down on hands and knees and crawled forward. Here was where the sentries had walked the last two nights. Tonight the ground ahead was empty. Blade moved to the left, toward a small fold in the ground. It gave him cover for a hundred yards. He crawled another hundred yards after that, then lay down to watch and listen again. The darkness was unbroken. The silence was not. Now he was close enough to hear the heavy snores of the sleeping men. They slept as though there were no possible danger within a hundred miles.

Certainly they were in no danger from him. Blade wanted Twana. He wouldn't lift a finger against any soldier who didn't interfere with that. If they all stayed asleep, they would all wake safely in the morning.

Blade rose on bare feet and padded forward, as alert and deadly as a prowling tiger. The sickle blade was thrust into his belt. In his left hand he carried the staff, in his right a loop of leather he'd picked up on the trail. The soldiers had discarded it as junk. To someone with Blade's skills, it was a perfect weapon for silent killing.

The tents and the wagons, the animals, and the sprawled blanket-wrapped forms on the ground grew larger. Blade swung around the end of the wagons. One of the riding animals raised its head and made a sizzling sound like grease in a frying pan. Blade froze. The sound drew an answering hiss from one of the wooden cages. The musky odor exhaled from the cages was strong in Blade's nostrils.

He didn't move until he was sure that the noise of the animals would not wake any of the sleeping men. Then he moved on. Before darkness fell, he'd counted the wagons. The women's wagons were fourth and fifth in line. He'd seen nine women taken out of them for dinner and an airing, Twana among them. He'd seen all nine put back before darkness fell.

He was passing the first wagon, and then the second. The third was coming up. Blade advanced one step at a time, lifting his feet carefully and setting them down still more carefully. He was passing the third wagon now. From just ahead he could hear the whimpering of some woman in a nightmare and smell faint hints of perfume.

Squeeee-eeee-eeeeyi! The sound was like a door closing on enormous rusty hinges, and it seemed to come almost from under Blade's feet. He froze, raised the staff, then looked down. A small ape-like animal was chained to the forward axle of the third wagon. Now it was jumping up and down and squealing like a nest of mice. Blade saw it hop up on the axle and draw breath to cry out again.

Blade didn't like the idea of killing someone's harmless pet, but the creature had to be silenced. He shifted his grip on the staff and struck downward. In the darkness his aim was off. The creature leaped nimbly down from the axle and darted away under the wagon to the full length of its chain.

From the other side of the wagon, Blade heard the sound of someone getting to his feet. He set his back against the wagon as two soldiers came stumbling around the end of it into view. From the way they moved and held their swords, Blade realized they were still half asleep.

He thrust his staff into the first soldier's throat. He felt the windpipe collapse under the blow, saw the man fall, and heard him choking as he thrashed on the ground. His comrade slashed at Blade, who stepped back and whirled his staff end for end. It smashed across the back of the soldier's neck, sending him forward on his face. Then the other end came

27

down with all of Blade's strength behind it, against the base of the soldier's skull. He died without a twitch or a whimper.

Both men were down, but the animal under the wagon was still piping shrilly. Blade could hear the snorts and curses of other soldiers rising out of sleep. He had even less time to waste than before.

He dashed to the fourth wagon, drew the sickle blade, and slashed at the curtains. After the first slash, he put the steel away and ripped with his bare hands. The curtains gaped open, and several women stuck their heads out to stare at Blade.

"Twana?" he called softly. Then, louder, "Twana!" A faint cry of surprise, then the sound of a struggle. A woman screamed; another sprawled on her stomach, half out of the wagon. Beside her, Twana's face appeared out of the darkness. Blade reached with both hands, clutched the girl by the shoulders, and heaved. With an astonished yelp, she flew out of the wagon. Blade's grip on her was all that kept her from sprawling on the ground.

She was barefoot and wore nothing but a length of cloth knotted about her waist. Even the quickest of glances told Blade that she was breathtakingly lovely, although shaking with cold, surprise, and fear. He snatched up a blanket dropped by one of the dead soldiers and ripped the shirt off the back of the other, then thrust both garments at Twana.

"Put these on and then *run!*"

"Run?" she repeated, her eyes wide and her hands trembling so that she could hardly grip the clothes.

"Yes, run!" said Blade. He would have liked to be gentle with the terrified girl, but there was no time. "Run toward the hills and the wall." He pointed into the darkness. "Find a spring at the foot of the hills and hide there."

"The Wall? It is forbidden. I cannot. . . ."

"If it's forbidden, then the soldiers won't think of looking for you there," said Blade. He felt like shouting. "Or do you want the soldiers to catch you again?"

That thought seemed to frighten Twana out of her paralysis. She snatched the garments from Blade's hands and dashed off into the darkness without bothering to put them on.

Blade hoped she'd be able to outrun any pursuers and wouldn't hide herself so thoroughly he couldn't find her himself. Meanwhile, a little quick work around the camp, and the soldiers might have too much on their minds to pursue him or Twana.

All the women in the two wagons started screaming at the top of their lungs. Blade couldn't make out a single word. He ignored them and bent to strip the dead soldiers of their weapons. He'd picked up a sword and was just picking up a bow when he saw two more soldiers coming at him out of the darkness.

Blade swung the bow sideways, cracking one man across the ankles. He yelped and began to dance around as if on hot bricks. Blade raised his sword and blocked the second man's thrust. The man's momentum carried him past Blade, who whirled and took his head off with a single slash. Blade slung the bow, picked up the quiver, and jumped onto the driver's seat of the nearest wagon. Now he could see more clearly what lay around him.

The camp was coming awake slowly, but too fast for Blade's comfort. He pulled an arrow from the quiver and looked for the two torches. If he could shoot them out, he'd have total darkness on his side. Then the musketeers and archers might not risk shooting for fear of hitting a friend.

Someone in the camp fired a musket, and someone else screamed in agony as the ball plowed into him. Blade found the first torch, aimed at it, and loosed his arrow. Someone ran into the circle of light around the torch just in time to take the arrow in his chest. Another scream tore the night, and a dying hand clutched the torch for a moment. Then the hand unfolded, and the torch dropped to the ground, going out as it struck.

Two arrows whistled over Blade's head; then a musket ball thudded into the wagon just below his feet. Some sharp-eyed soul had apparently picked him out as the source of the trouble in the camp.

Blade sprang down from the wagon seat, slung his bow, and charged into the camp. That was the last place anybody would think of looking for him at the moment. He ran until he felt as if he were skimming the ground, leaping over tent cords and men still wrapped in their blankets. As he approached the second torch, he saw a group of four men burst out from the tents, heading in the same direction. They reached the torch first. As the man in the lead clutched it, Blade recognized him. It was the Aygoon.

Blade didn't even break stride. He was on the men before they could even see him coming. They wore no armor. Blade's sword swung, taking two of the men in a single slash. One clapped his hands over a gaping chest; the other gushed blood where his jaw had been. They fell back, driving the third man with them. Blade turned to face the Aygoon.

The Aygoon started to drop the torch, raising his sword with his free hand. Before he could complete either movement, Blade's left hand closed on the shaft of the torch. Blade's enormous strength snatched the torch away as if the Aygoon had been a child. The man struck a desperately clumsy, one-handed blow with his sword. Blade blocked it easily, then thrust the torch into the Aygoon's face. His beard and hair blazed up. He dropped his sword with a scream and clawed at his face. Blade put an end to the Aygoon's agony by splitting his skull with an overhand slash. Then Blade turned and ran, bloody sword in one hand and torch blazing in the other.

He didn't throw the torch away. A plan had leaped into his mind. If he carried out that plan, not only he and Twana, but Twana's village, might be safe from the Shoba's soldiers.

On the far side of the camp lay the five cannon and the canvas-covered wagons that held their powder and shot. Blade charged across the camp toward those wagons as if he were trying to set an Olympic record. The torch danced and flickered wildly but kept burning. Arrows and musket balls whistled past him in all directions. Everyone in the camp seemed to be in a panic of firing. None of the shots came close to Blade, but he heard a number of screams as men hit their own comrades. With their commanding officer dead, it might be quite a while before even the best-trained soldiers got themselves sorted out.

Blade ran past the cannon and up to the first of the wagons. He yanked off the cover and saw a pile of canvas bags. They bulged as if they held shot. Not what he wanted. He moved on to the next wagon.

A bullet whistled inches from his ear as he tore the cover off the second wagon and saw a dozen fat wooden barrels, all heavily tarred. A large wooden mallet lay in the bottom of the wagon. Blade picked it up, as another musket ball flew so close he felt the wind on his skin. Two sharp blows, and the wood of the barrel's head cracked. Black grains trickled out. Blade thrust the torch against the canvas cover, waited until the flames began to rise, then threw the canvas over the barrels. The tar took fire. Blade threw the torch in among the barrels and ran, as arrows began to whistle down around him. He ran off into the darkness, and he'd covered about two hundred yards before the power wagon exploded.

The sheet of flame seemed to wash over the whole camp, and Blade saw tents go down and wagons topple over as if they'd been shoved by a giant hand. Bits and pieces of flaming wreckage shot into the air like fireworks. Then the long rumble and roar of the explosion surrounded him. The shock wave was so violent he nearly stumbled. He kept on until the last of the flames died. Then he slowed down and made a wide half-circle around to the other side of the camp, where the animals were tethered.

By that time some of the soldiers were mounting up. The first few had just climbed into their saddles when Blade's arrows came slicing down out of the darkness. He was firing almost blind, but the mass of tethered animals and men working around them made a target impossible to miss.

He shot eleven arrows, leaving him with a dozen in the quiver. He couldn't see who or what he was hitting, but he heard a good many screams and cries, both human and animal. Hitting even half a dozen animals would probably throw the rest into such a panic that it would be hours before anyone could ride them. During those hours he and Twana could build up a long lead.

Then the soldiers might well decide to abandon the chase. They'd even have trouble taking vengeance on Twana's village. Without powder, their cannon and muskets would be useless.

31

Without the cannon and muskets, the villagers could put up a good fight from behind their stone walls.

As he slung his bow and headed south, Blade felt he'd done a good night's work. Now all that remained was to find Twana and return her safely to Hores.

Chapter 5

Blade ran until the last sight and sound of the camp faded into the night. Then he slowed down to a steady lope that he could keep up all night if he had to.

He kept on the move for an hour until he reached a small pond. He drank from the pond until he was no longer thirsty, then started off again. He kept moving the rest of the night, stopping every hour or so to catch his breath and listen for any sounds of pursuit. Once he must have stopped close to a village, for he heard the bleating of goats in the distance. Otherwise he heard nothing except his own breathing and an occasional night insect.

Blade's spirits rose as he moved along. If the Shoba's men wanted to have any hope of catching him, they'd better sort themselves out and hurry up! If they didn't hurry, they'd have a hard time picking up his fast-cooling trail, even mounted.

Still, Blade was not the sort to write off an enemy until he'd buried the man with his own hands. He'd be even more careful about a party of trained soldiers, some of whom at least would certainly keep their heads.

Blade was still on the move when dawn broke. He found himself barely a mile from the foot of the hills, which rose even more steeply here than where he'd seen them the evening before. The wall still ran along the crest, as though it would go on to the end of the world and a mile beyond. Whatever it was made of still showed an even blue-grayness, with no detail at all.

It was full daylight before Blade came to another spring. This one had made a small pool between two rocky spurs jutting out from the hills. Blade stopped, drank, then stripped off his clothes and plunged into the pool. He ignored the bone-chilling cold as he scrubbed off the sweat, grime, and dried blood from his night's work. Then he ran around in circles to dry off and warm up, dressed, and started to climb one of the rocky spurs.

The wall itself could wait. Right now he wanted to look for signs of pursuit and signs of Twana. He scrambled upward until the plain was nearly five hundred feet below. In spite of the slope, the rock was rough enough to be easy climbing. It seemed to go on like that all the way up to the base of the wall. Even Twana should be able to climb the hills without too much trouble, if that turned out to be necessary.

From his perch Blade could see no trace of Twana. To balance that disappointment, he could also see no sign of the Shoba's men. They seemed to have vanished from the face of the land. Far off toward the north, he saw a faint hint of movement along the foot of the hills. Whatever it was, it was far too small and slow moving to be the column of soldiers and wagons. Probably a village's flocks being driven out to pasture for the day.

So much for the Shoba's men. Blade put them out of his mind and scrambled down toward the plain to begin his search for Twana.

He found her a little after noon, huddled in the shadow of a clump of bushes by the mouth of a small cave just above the level of the plain. A stream flowed out of the cave and across the plain, toward a village about three miles away. Blade wondered why Twana hadn't sought out food and warmth in the village, instead of sitting here shivering and alone.

Blade held the girl until she stopped shaking with cold and the relief from fear and strain. He stroked her hair and cheeks, kissed her on the eyes, made soothing and reassuring noises, but did nothing more. He was very conscious of her warmth and graceful beauty, but he was even more conscious of the fear that filled her. It would be a long time before this girl wanted anything but a reassuring, protecting presence from a man. He would see that she got that.

At last Blade thought Twana might to ready to speak. "Twana. Are you hurt? Can you walk a little farther?"

She turned enormous brown eyes toward him. "How—how do you know my name?"

Blade decided to tell the girl the truth. "When the Shoba's men came to Hores, I was hiding in a place nearby. I could see everything that happened and hear much, even your name."

"You—you saw the Shoba's men, the iron dragons, the beating of Naran, my father?"

"I said I saw everything that happened at your village, Twana. That is why I came to the camp of the Shoba's men at night, to fight them and help you escape."

Twana shivered more violently than before. Blade put his arms around her again. "Come, Twana. I think we should go to that village that I see only an hour away. You need food and warmth that I cannot give you out here."

Instead of seeming relieved or happy at the idea, Twana shuddered again and shook her head furiously. "No. It will be death for them if we go there. We cannot go there."

"How is that, Twana? I have destroyed the powder they put in the iron dragons to make them throw stones at villages. I have frightened their riding animals. I have killed the Aygoon of the Tribute himself. I cannot imagine that they will even come after us now. Even if they come after us, how can they find us, or learn that we have gone to the village?"

Twana's face turned the color of milk, and she sat down as if her legs had turned to jelly. Slowly she shook her head. "How can you say these things, unless you are mad or . . . ?"

"I am not mad, Twana. Do not worry about that. My name is Blade, and I am from a distant land, where not much is known of the Shoba's men. Perhaps you can tell me things that I should know about them?"

Twana's words came out in a rush. "The Shoba's men will come after us. They are too strong to be beaten by what you have done. They will find someone to give orders like the Aygoon. They will tame their animals again. They may be on our trail now."

"Perhaps. But how can they pick up our trail when we have come so far?"

"You do not know of the sniffers then?"

"What are they? Men or animals?"

The sniffers of the Shoba had apparently been a frightful menace among Twana's people for so long that trying to describe them frightened her almost speechless. Blade had to be continually prompting her and make his own guesses about things she would not discuss. Gradually he understood what a sniffer was and why Twana and her people were frightened of it. He had to admit that fear seemed justified.

A sniffer sounded like a cross between a centipede and a porcupine, but it was the size of a small pony. It was covered from throat to tail with two-foot spines. Their sense of smell was incredibly acute. If a sniffer were given any article that had ever belonged to a person to smell, it could trail that person over any kind of country for a week or more. When it caught up with its prey, it would close in rapidly on its thirty-eight legs and hold the person at bay, or even kill, with swings of the four-foot tail. The spines on the tail were poisonous.

"Do the Shoba's men have something that you wore?" asked Blade.

Twana nodded. "They took all my clothes before they put me in the wagon with the other women." She shuddered. "Most of them were pleasure slaves for the Aygoon and his men. They beat me with silk cords and made me wait on them. One of them was an *uldao*—a woman who loves women instead of men. She made me. . . ." She could not go on, but clung to Blade until the memories faded.

Finally she stepped away from him. After several deep breaths, she seemed to gain a good deal of self-control. "The soldiers have more than enough to send the sniffers after me. But they do not have anything of yours, so the sniffers will not be after you. You should go on alone and leave me. You have struck a mighty blow against the Shoba, and I am grateful. But there is no need for you to die by torture. You must. . . ."

Blade pressed his fingers across her lips to silence her. "No, Twana. I will not do it that way. I will stay with you. Whatever danger comes after you will also come after me. Two people can guard themselves better than one."

36

"Not with the sniffers. . . ."

"Yes, even with the sniffers on their trail. Now, let us talk no more of this." He was about to say, "If all else fails, we can go over the wall where the sniffers can hardly follow us." Then he remembered that Twana was apparently in terror of the wall. There was no point in reawakening fear in her now.

"All right," said Twana. "We shall go on. But let us not go to this village, either of us. If we go in daylight, certainly they will see us. The Shoba's men will come, and they will punish the village for helping us. They will punish the village even without the iron dragons, by killing their animals or cutting down their trees or throwing dung down their wells."

"Then we'll go on to the next village and wait until dark. I'll slip in and get what we need, while you keep watch for the Shoba's men and the sniffers."

Twana nodded jerkily. Blade seemed to have convinced her that there was something to do against the Shoba's men beside curling up and dying. Now that she accepted this, she seemed to be gaining courage and determination with each passing moment.

Blade looked at the sky. It was time that he and Twana moved on, to take advantage of the remaining daylight. He took her hand and led her away toward the south.

Chapter 6

They reached another village as the sun was setting. This village had a wall of mud brucks topped with wooden stakes, but there were huts scattered around the pastures and along the shores of a small lake. These promised easier pickings for Blade, without getting the villagers aroused and on his trail.

Blade and Twana waited in the shadows at the foot of the hills until darkness came. The girl was obviously still nervous about being this close to the Wall—the way she said the word made the capital *W* obvious to Blade's ears. She kept looking upward, as though expecting something to leap down upon them from above. Once Blade saw another gleam of metal on top of the Wall, but it was miles away, and he could make out no details in the fading light.

Darkness came, and Blade went to work. With Twana keeping watch outside, he carefully went through each hut. By the time he'd finished, he had clothes, footgear, blankets, and knives, for both himself and Twana. He even found a goatskin water bottle and a long rope. He only stopped because there was no point in taking more than he could carry away.

They moved on through the darkness until the last faint trace of light from the village was lost behind them. At last, they came to a patch of low, spreading bushes and crawled in under them. Neither men nor sniffers could come at them now without giving warning of their approach and waking Blade.

Blade spread one blanket on the ground under them, then drew Twana close with one arm and pulled the rest of the blankets over them with the other. Gradually the blankets and their closely nestled bodies drove away the chill of the night. Gradually Blade also became aware of another kind of warmth growing in him. It was inevitable with Twana's supple, graceful body pressing so closely against his. It was also something he would do his best to fight. After her experiences of the past few days, sex was probably the farthest thing in the whole world from Twana's mind. Blade tried to pillow his head as comfortably as possible on a rolled-up fur hood and found himself drifting off to sleep. He'd been awake for nearly two solid days and on the move most of the time. Even his iron frame needed a rest.

Twana also seemed to be falling asleep. Her eyes drifted shut, and her breathing became slow and regular. One arm was thrown out across Blade's massive chest.

Just as he was drifting off to sleep, Blade realized that Twana's hand had begun to move with what seemed a life of its own. Her eyes were still closed, but her fingers were creeping down across his ribs, stroking the tanned skin and feeling for the layers of hard muscle under it. Those fingers were very gentle, but very sure in their movements. The erotic warmth began to grow again in Blade.

Twana sighed and, without opening her eyes, pressed her cheek against Blade's side. He raised a hand and stroked her hair. Twana made a small sound that was halfway between a sigh and a giggle and pressed herself harder against Blade. Her hand now crept down over Blade's stomach, then dipped between his legs.

Blade gave a husky laugh. Apparently the last few days hadn't driven all thoughts of sex out of Twana's mind after all! The warmth he'd felt was beginning to center in his groin, and his breathing quickened as Twana's hand continued its travels.

Then her fingers closed with delicate firmness on his manhood, and suddenly he was swollen, erect, ready, with desire almost boiling over in him. He gasped and rolled toward the girl. She gave a long "Ahhhhhhh!" and threw both arms around him as they rolled together. Blade's lips sought Twana's and found them, while his hands cupped the small, firm breasts. The nipples had risen into long, almost jutting

40

points that were as firm as if they'd been something more than warm woman's flesh.

They caressed and kissed and pressed against each other for what seemed hours, but could only have been minutes. Twana's breath was coming so quickly and so hard that Blade could hear her over his own gasps. The mouth under his was warm, almost hot, wet, demanding and seeking, but also giving generously at the same time.

Twana whispered and rolled over on her back. As she did, she clamped her hands in Blade's hair and drew his head down with almost painful force to bring his lips to her breasts. He was more than happy to keep his lips there, and his tongue as well. The nipples and the lovely breasts around them seemed to grow warm themselves under his kisses and caresses.

Then the flame in Blade's groin was blazing so fiercely that he could no longer hold himself back from trying to quench it. He raised himself until the muscles in his arms stood out in knots and cords. Twana saw him above her and saw that the moment had come. Her legs drifted apart, and she thrust her pelvis with its triangle of damp hair up toward Blade. He lunged downward, and it seemed to him that they met in midair and flew away together into the night sky. Never before had his first moment of entry into a woman brought such an overpowering assault on his senses.

The feeling was so powerful that it was almost terrifying. Blade clung to Twana, not only in passion, but in the need to hold on to some part of the real world. She clutched him in an even greater frenzy, and he could feel her shaking as he moved within her.

He moved slowly at first, although it cost him a heroic effort at self-restraint. If he'd let himself go, he would have taken Twana with a desperate fury certain to frighten her half out of her wits. So he was gentle, almost delicate. Gradually he felt Twana's movements rise to match his and then move beyond them. Under the fear there was a core of passion in her, and he was reaching it.

Blade threw off all restraint and no longer held himself back. He no longer needed to, and he couldn't have done so even if he'd wanted to. Twana clutched him tighter and began to moan.

Suddenly the moans turned into a shrill scream. Twana writhed and twisted, her mouth pouring out wild, meaningless sounds, her legs clamped tight around Blade and her nails raking his back. He could feel her twisting within as well, as every part of her body threw itself into a wild convulsion of released desire.

Then Twana's convulsion drew Blade up to his own peak and pushed him over. She cried out again as she felt him pouring himself hotly into her, and a third time as his arms tightened around her like steel bands. Then Blade was sagging down on her, as though all his strength had poured out of him along with all his desire. His head came to rest between Twana's breasts, and her hands drifted down to rest lightly in his tangled hair.

It was a while before they found the strength to untangle themselves long enough to pull the blankets over them. Even that strength didn't last long. Both of them were asleep within a few minutes, and it didn't matter whether the Shoba's men and sniffers were one mile away or a thousand.

They lay snugly together until just before dawn. Then Blade woke, crept out from the blankets without waking the sleeping girl, and drank some water. He woke Twana, and together they collected their gear and headed toward the hills.

Twana's face grew more strained as the hills and the Wall on top loomed higher and higher above them. She stayed quiet until they'd reached the very foot of the nearest hill. Blade unslung his pack and turned toward the slope, and that drew a wild cry from her.

"No, Blade! Do not! You must not go up there! The Watchers will take you. You must not die and leave me alone!"

Blade turned. This seemed as good a time as any to find out what made Twana so fearful of the hills and the Wall. "What are the Watchers, Twana, that a warrior needs to be afraid of them? The Shoba's men found me hard to kill. Why should the Watchers have it any easier?"

"You do not understand, Blade. The Watchers who defend

42

the Wall are not men. You are strong against men, but. . . ."

Blade held up a hand to interrupt her. "The Watchers are not men? Then what are they?"

Twana swallowed. "It—they—no one can say for sure. Those who could know—they are dead. The Watchers killed them."

"How?"

Once more Blade had to piece together a picture out of Twana's disjointed answers to a series of questions. When he'd finished, he understood why the Watchers of the Wall, like the Shoba's sniffers, were something to be feared.

The Wall had marched along the crests of the hills to the west as far back as the memory of Twana's people went. During all that time, it had been protected by the Watchers. These were not men, but great monsters that seemed to have something of the shape of a man. They were many times the size of the largest man though. They moved in ways no living creature ever could, and they shone all over as if they were made of metal.

They caught and killed anyone who came too close to the Wall. This was certain, for they had been seen to do it. No one knew exactly how they killed or why, but it was certain that they did. No one who had gone up to the base of the Wall had ever come back down. Even the Shoba's men would not go where they might have to face the invincible Watchers. They would not even light fires or post sentries when they were close to the Wall, for fear of drawing the anger of the Watchers.

Twana's story of the Watchers still further aroused Blade's curiosity. Like the Wall itself, the Watchers hinted at an advanced civilization lying somewhere to the west. Unlike the Wall, which could have stood a thousand years after the last of its builders vanished, the Watchers suggested that civilization still survived.

For the moment this would make no difference to Blade's plans. He would cheerfully risk his own neck many times over to satisfy his curiosity, but he would not put Twana in danger if he could avoid it. They would continue their flight

43

as if the Wall and the Watchers didn't exist, until either they were safe or the Shoba's men overtook them.

"Very well. We shall not go near the Wall unless the Shoba's men are about to catch us. Then we will go up the hill and take our chances with the Watchers."

"But. . . ."

"Twana, the Shoba's men will kill us when they catch us, won't they?" She nodded, shuddering. "Then what do we have to lose? Even if the Watchers do kill us, it will surely be a quicker, cleaner death than the Shoba's men would give us. And who knows? The Watchers may not kill us after all. Perhaps the men who went up to the Wall found a rich land, with beautiful women and rivers of beer. They didn't come back because they didn't want to." It was a feeble joke, but enough to make Twana smile. She was still smiling as Blade turned to the slope and began scrambling upward.

The smile died swiftly when he returned, his face set as hard as the rocks of the hillside. "They are coming after us, aren't they?" she said.

"Yes. Mounted men, light carts, and two things that move low along the ground."

The sniffers. Neither of them said the word, because it wasn't necessary. Blade had a brief, bleak moment of realizing that Twana had been right. If the Shoba's men had been willing to follow this far, they were not easily discouraged. If the sniffers could follow such a faint trail, they were as good as Twana said they were. The odds were not good.

They weren't hopeless either. If the Shoba's men weren't easily discouraged, neither was Blade. Sniffers might have supernatural powers of scent, but not after they were dead. If all else failed, there was still the Wall.

Blade slung his pack and took Twana's hand. The chase was on again, deadlier than before.

Chapter 7

The next three days were exhausting, but also a challenge to Blade's skill and experience. He could almost have enjoyed it if Twana hadn't been with him and if the stakes hadn't been so high. If they were caught, the best they could hope for was a swift death.

Blade used every trick that he'd ever learned and a few he made up on the spot. He sought out the rockiest ground, where there was nothing to show a footprint or hold a scent. He zigzagged and doubled back whenever he could afford the time and distance. He marched for miles in his bare feet, carrying Twana on his back. He led the chase through every stream and pond that was shallow enough to wade. Once they even took off their clothes and swam a mile down a small river. Another time they came to a stand of trees that grew close together. They climbed the nearest tree and covered several hundred yards by swinging from branch to branch, like Tarzan of the Apes. They did everything except walk on their hands, and Blade would have done that if possible.

It was not enough.

The sniffers never lost the trail, at least not for more than an hour or two. Every time Blade climbed the hill to look to the north, the Shoba's men were a little bit closer.

Fortunately, the enemy could only pursue at the speed of the sniffers. The sniffers could move only a little faster than a man on foot, and there were only two of them. They had tremendous endurance though—like machines of steel and rubber, rather than creatures of flesh and blood. Slowly the gap between the pursuers and the pursued closed.

On the evening of the third day, Blade knew that he and

Twana had reached the end of their running. Their pursuers were so close that sometimes he could hear the high-pitched whistling cries of the green riding animals, the druns. Fortunately, the ground was turning rugged, cut up with low hills and ravines that provided plenty of cover. Without that cover, the enemy would long since have been able to charge forward and ride down their prey with no further help from the sniffers.

Blade knew that in another day or two he and Twana would no longer be able to afford the time to sleep at night. Then exhaustion would bring them down swiftly and make them an easy, even helpless, prey for their pursuers.

Fight or climb the Wall? The Wall was still with them, although they must have come more than a hundred miles from where Blade first saw it. A half-hour's brisk climbing, and they would be at its base. Then Blade could climb any of the overgrown stretches and haul Twana up with the rope. He'd worry about the Watchers when and if he had to.

Blade decided to fight. "They seem to be only twelve men and two sniffers," he said. "Even if we do not kill all the men, we may kill the sniffers, and then the men will have to give up the pursuit. There are no other men of the Shoba for many miles around. Then we can stop running, regain our strength, and return north to Hores.

"I will go in at night," he went on. "Even if they have some warning from the sniffers, I won't be an easy target. Also, they may be slow to use arrows or guns in the camp for fear of hitting friends."

"Yes," said Twana. "While you fight, I can creep close to the druns and cut them loose, so they will run off."

Blade opened his mouth to tell the girl she wouldn't be anywhere near the fight, but she shook her head firmly. "No, Blade. I will not sit in the darkness and hear you die. I can cut the druns loose. I can watch your back. I can set fire to the tents. I cannot fight a soldier of the Shoba as you can, but I can kill those you have wounded. We do not want to leave any of them alive if we can." There was chill hatred in those last words, a hatred built up over many generations and now entirely sweeping away her fear. "We are together in

46

this, Blade. We must be. We must be together in this battle as we were in the love we shared last night."

Blade swore mentally, but there was a smile on his face. Such courage moved him. Twana would hardly be in more danger coming with him than staying behind, and an extra pair of eyes and hands would be useful.

"Very well, together," he said, and kissed her.

The night was totally black, and a brisk north wind blew stinging dust into Blade's eyes. Since he would be coming up on the enemy camp from the south, the wind would blow his scent away from the sniffers and any sound he might make away from the ears of the sentries.

Blade reached out and ran his fingers over Twana's face. She was almost invisible in the darkness. Like Blade, she had put on her darkest clothing and then rubbed dirt on her hands and face. They would be as hard to see as black cats, and Blade hoped they could move as silently.

They crept forward. The wind brought them the cries of the tethered druns, but no human voices. There were certain to be sentries posted, but not many. With surprise and darkness on his side, Blade was certain he could take care of these before their comrades could wake.

The approach to the camp seemed to take hours, although they had barely a mile to cover. Blade was half-expecting dawn to appear in the eastern sky before they reached striking range of the camp.

From the hillside the evening before, Blade had watched the enemy settling down for the night. He'd carefully noted the lay of the land and the best approach to the camp. Now he led Twana behind a low rise in the ground, just high enough to conceal them. Twana lay still while Blade crept out into the open. After a while, his night vision could make out the dim shapes of the druns and the wagon that held the sniffers. He could also make out three sentries. No tents, no fire. As before, the Shoba's men would not light a fire this close to the Wall and its Watchers.

Blade twisted on to his side and drew an arrow from his quiver. Then he sprang to his feet and, in almost the same motion, aimed, drew and let fly. The arrow whistled through fifty yards of wind-whipped night air to find a target in the sentry's chest. He was dying before his ears registered the whistle of the arrow that killed him. Blade nocked a second arrow. The second sentry turned toward him, and the man's white face gave him a fine aiming point. The man died with a gurgling scream.

The scream startled the druns into shrill cries and alerted the third sentry on the far side of the camp. He raised his musket and let fly with a thundering crash and a flare of orange-red flame. His ball sailed off into the night, but the noise brought every man in the camp awake.

Blade shot a third arrow into the men as they kicked themselves free of their blankets. Then he dropped the bow and drew both sword and knife.

"Get the animals," he called to Twana and ran forward. He knew without hearing or seeing her that she was running forward with him, knife in hand. Now it would be all close-quarters fighting, where Blade's strength and speed would be deadly and the enemy's bows and muskets useless.

A soldier came at Blade, trying to cut between him and the animals. The man wore only boots and breechclout but carried sword and shield. His sword whistled at Blade's head. Blade savagely parried the cut with his knife. Sparks sprayed down, and the man was a little slow in drawing back his arm. Blade thrust his knife deep into the flesh of that arm, then swung his sword. The man's throat gaped wide as though he'd suddenly opened a second, blood-gushing mouth.

One of the druns screamed, in pain this time. Twana was at work with her knife. Another man came at Blade, this one carrying shield and a single-handed axe. He used both of them skillfully, forcing Blade to give ground. Blade would have liked to close and kill the man, but he knew he couldn't afford to let himself be held in any one place for long. That would give the others time to surround him and put their superior numbers to work.

Blade kept backing, until he realized he was in danger of being backed right out of the camp, leaving Twana alone. He charged, swinging around to the left of the axeman, faster than the other could turn, then closing in. He stabbed the man in the groin with his knife and hacked his weapons arm nearly free of the shoulder. The man reeled back, dropping his axe. Blade snatched it up, looked for Twana's slim figure darting about among the animals, saw her. He raised the axe, shouted "Get this!", and threw it. The axe would be a good weapon for killing the sniffers.

Now Twana had released one of the druns and prodded it into a panic-stricken flight. It charged through the camp, nearly knocking Blade flat. He leaped clear in time, got his feet tangled in someone's discarded blankets, went down, rolled with expert skill, and came up still armed and ready.

His opponent's weren't quite so fortunate. The maddened drun knocked two of them flat and brought the rest to a standstill. Before they could recover, Blade charged.

He leaped over one of the fallen men and came down on the chest of the other in an explosive crackling of shattered ribs. He leaped down to the ground as the man went into a final blood-spraying convulsion. His sword cut the air in a flat arc and took a head off its shoulders. The corpse toppled almost at Blade's feet. He stepped behind it, keeping two more men at a distance great enough to spoil their attack. Their swords lashed out. Blade parried one with his knife, immobilizing it. He lopped off the hand that held the other sword, then turned back to the first man.

As he did, Twana screamed in raw terror. Blade smashed the shield of the man facing him with a brutal downcut, laid open his chest with a second cut, and backed away as the man fell. Now he could clearly see Twana and why she'd screamed.

One of the sniffers was loose. Twana was backed against the wagon, shaking with fear as she stared wildly at the creature in front of her. Every time she moved so much as a finger, the deadly spine-studded tail waved toward her. Every time the poisoned tips stopped inches from her skin. At other times the sniffer opened its mouth and hissed angrily. The mouth was full of teeth, chisel-shaped like a beaver's—long and sharp enough to do plenty of damage if they sank into human flesh. Twana's axe lay on the ground at her feet, its head dark with blood.

Blade's sword chopped into the base of the sniffer's spine. The poisoned tail lashed wildly back toward him, so hard

49

that some of the spines raked across his boots. They left dark, oozing lines across the leather but didn't penetrate to the skin. Then the tail flopped limply to the ground as the sniffer lost control of it. Half mad with pain, it turned to face Blade, and Blade's sword came down across the back of its neck. The sniffer dropped nose first to the ground and lay there, quivering all over. It made noises so much like the cries of a kitten that Blade was relieved when Twana picked up the axe and brought it down hard, ending the sniffer's death agony.

Then she was dropping the axe and clinging desperately to his left arm. Gently he shook her loose and turned to face his remaining human enemies. After a long moment's staring into the darkness around him, he realized there weren't any in sight.

Instantly Blade's mind conjured up a picture of the Shoba's men backing away until they could fill him and Twana with arrows, with little danger to themselves. He grabbed Twana by the wrist and dragged her with him under the sniffer's wagon. They lay flat, eyes searching the darkness for any sign of the enemy, ears listening for the whistle of descending arrows.

He heard and saw nothing. He whispered to Twana, "What about the other sniffer?"

"I killed it with the axe before the other one came at me." He could feel her shivering. The generations-old terror of the Shoba's sniffers was still in her.

Blade waited, but gradually he began to suspect there was nothing to wait for. With both their sniffers dead, the rest of the Shoba's men might have decided they had no chance anymore of carrying out their mission. The best course would be to clear out, try to run down their scattered druns, and then ride to rejoin their comrades.

Blade wondered, in spite of this. The Shoba's men could still have made a good try at killing him while he was busy with the sniffer. As far as he knew, they hadn't lifted a finger. They'd just vanished into the night. It wasn't what he would have expected from soldiers who'd shown themselves so tough and determined.

Slowly Blade crawled out from under the wagon. When

this drew no shouts or arrows, he called softly to Twana. She scrambled out with frantic haste, and together they searched the camp. Blade gathered up two more knives, a sword, and a spare bow. He packed his quiver full of arrows, but decided against picking up a musket. It would be far too heavy in proportion to its range and striking power, and useless when its powder ran out.

Meanwhile, Twana had been collecting pouches of dried meat and hard biscuit scattered among the blankets. They were a welcome find, one that promised better eating on the way north. But why had the soldiers abandoned them? And it made no sense for them to abandon the food . . . ?

Oh well. Blade decided to put the matter of the strange behavior of the Shoba's soldiers out of his mind. He knew he was only guessing—always a waste of time when he knew so little for certain.

At last Blade led Twana out of the camp. He wanted to get well away from it and then under cover, in case one or two of the soldiers might have the courage to return. A night's sleep, a quick climb up the hill to make sure the enemy was really gone, and they could start back toward Hores. Once there, he could leave Twana and get about his real business in this Dimension, which was now the Wall and whatever might lie beyond it.

They slept behind some squat trees, so close to the foot of the hills that the ground already sloped upward. Blade and Twana had to brace themselves against gnarled roots, and against each other, to keep from rolling down the slope into a pond.

At dawn they rose, filled their water bottles, and climbed the hill together. Blade was happy that Twana had found the courage to climb up with him. If she returned to her village with some of the terror of the Wall shaken out of her mind, it might be a good thing for her people.

They had to climb farther than usual to get above the morning mist. At last they climbed into clear air and looked to the north. Blade looked for a long time—then his angry words echoed around the rocky hillside, until Twana stared at him as if he'd gone mad. Then he started to laugh, and she stared even more. She was beginning to look frightened, when Blade threw out one arm and pointed to the north.

"Look again, Twana!"

She did so and saw what Blade had seen. Moving steadily south on their trail was another party of the Shoba's soldiers. In this one there were at least thirty men, as many druns, and no less than five sniffers.

Blade stopped laughing. "I can see what they must have done. They must have been sending the men we fought on ahead by day. The others stayed well behind and probably moved only by night, when we couldn't have seen them even if we'd been looking for them. That's why the soldiers ran away last night. They knew they had some place to run to. Now they're back on our trail again." He didn't add that this seemed to be the second time he'd badly underestimated the Shoba's men.

Aloud, he went on. "There are too many of them for us to fight, I'm afraid. We either stay down here and die, or climb up to the Wall and let the Watchers do their worst."

Twana shivered, but her voice was steady as she replied, "The Wall. I do not know for certain what the Watchers can do. I know the Shoba's men."

They began their climb to the Wall.

Chapter 8

They climbed in as nearly a straight line as they could manage. Blade wanted to get high above the plain and well out of bowshot before the second party of pursuers caught up with them.

This stretch of hillside was steeper than most and also booby trapped with loose slabs of rock. In spite of the occasional falls and scraped skin, Blade was happy about the difficult slope. The Shoba's heavily equipped soldiers would have a slow and painful time tackling the hillside. In the process, they would make fine targets of themselves for a man waiting above with a bow and a large supply of arrows.

This hill was also higher than usual—in fact, it almost deserved the name of mountain. The base of the Wall was nearly half a mile above the plain. Long before Blade and Twana reached it, the Shoba's men had ridden up to the foot of the hill. After they'd proved to their own satisfaction that they were out of range, with a few useless musket shots and arrows, they settled down to wait. Blade felt a moment's temptation to thumb his nose at the enemy. They would have a *long* wait for him and Twana to come down. The temptation vanished swiftly as he looked upward to the endless grim Wall that loomed steadily closer with each step they took.

At last there was no more upward slope in front of them. Far below the Shoba's men looked like ants crawling about on the plain. Directly above them rose the Wall, so close that Blade could reach out and touch it. The blue-gray material was cold, as hard as metal, and faintly rough to the touch, like fine sandpaper. Here and there in the blue-grayness, Blade could see faint swirling patterns, but he could see no seams or cracks. The technology that had built the Wall was certainly far ahead of Home Dimension. More than ever, Blade was curious to see what lay beyond the Wall. What would the builders have considered so valuable that they would build this Wall along a hundred or more miles of hill crest to protect it? Or what danger was so great that the Wall was needed to guard against it?

All along the base of the Wall, shrubs and vines crept upward in thick, tangled clumps, as if the presence of the Wall made the soil at its base more fertile than elsewhere on the hills. Blade and Twana started north, while Blade looked for a vine or tree strong enough and tall enough to carry him to the top of the Wall. Twana kept an eye out for the Watchers. She was pale and moved with little jerky steps, as though she expected the Watchers to rise out of the ground in front of her at any moment. But she was also alert and kept up well.

In an hour they'd left the Shoba's men out of sight in the haze and mist to the south. Twana was beginning to mutter, "Where are the Watchers?" Blade would have liked an answer to the same question. Here they are, marching steadily along the very base of the Wall, without the faintest sign that the Watchers even existed. If the legends were entirely true, they should have been dead by now.

Somebody else had risked the Watchers, a long time in the past. Blade saw a place where at least a ton of gunpowder must have been set off against the base of the Wall. The rock was split and shattered, and a blackened hole revealed several feet of the Wall's foundations. The Wall itself showed a faint discoloration and some barely visible pitting, but otherwise the explosion had left it completely unaffected.

Another hour's walking brought Blade and Twana to a stretch of Wall three hundred yards long and completely overgrown with massive vines from ground level all the way to the top. A six-year-old child could have scrambled up those vines, let alone a trained athlete like Blade, who had climbed the face of the Eiger.

He went up carefully though. He weighted a good deal more than any six-year-old child. If the vines did break under him, he might be dropped forty or fifty feet onto hard rock.

54

A broken leg here and now could be a good deal more fatal than the Watchers.

Foot by foot, Blade clambered upward. In places his fingers pushed through the tangle of vines and touched the Wall itself. When he did that, he could feel a faint, irregular vibration within the blue-gray material. It was like putting his fingers on the head of an enormous drum being gently tapped by an invisible drummer. Once he was able to put his ear against the Wall and hear a distant humming that came and went in irregular pulses. The Wall was not as dead as it seemed, or perhaps even as solid.

The last few feet were particularly tricky. The vines were growing thinner, the twice strands broke as Blade gripped them. Both times he hung there with a death clutch on the broken strands, barely breathing, toes curling for a better foothold.

At last there was no more Wall to climb, only a flat surface like a blue-gray tabletop stretching out of sight. The golden shimmering in the air above the Wall was clearly visible now. It seemed to start three or four feet above the top and then curve upward and away toward the inner side of the Wall. It was soundless, odorless, unchanging, and totally unlike anything Blade had ever seen or imagined. It reminded him that, as he explored the Wall, he might be in the position of a caveman trying to examine and understand a jet bomber —or an atomic reactor.

Blade scrambled out onto the top of the Wall. On hands and knees he crawled forward. He held his sword in one hand, probing the featureless surface ahead of him as he moved.

He covered forty feet, and then suddenly he could no longer see. It was as if he'd stuck his head into a black sack. He drew back, startled, and vision instantly returned. He looked ahead, at both the Wall and the air above it. High above he caught hints of the golden shimmering. Directly in front of him, he could see nothing at all except the top of the Wall. He crawled forward—and again the world vanished around him.

He tried three more times, until his head was beginning to spin with the repeated coming and going of his vision. By that time he realized what had to be wrong. The Wall was generating some sort of field that completely deprived him of vision. That field started at a point only a yard or so in front of him and continued until . . . ?

That was a question he'd have to answer, sooner or later. Not now though. Not when he had Twana to get back home and the Shoba's men were still close enough to take advantage of any mistakes he might make. He crawled back to the edge of the Wall and stood up slowly. As his head rose into the golden shimmering, he had a moment's sensation of being jabbed with thousands of tiny blunt needles. Then the sensation faded. Whatever the shimmering meant, it did not appear to be dangerous.

Blade tied a loop in the end of the rope and threw the loop down to Twana. She caught it and drew it around her body. Then Blade began to back slowly away from the edge of the Wall, pulling Twana up as he did.

He was also keeping watch on either side of him, along the top of the Wall. It rose and fell in long, slow curves, like waves far out at sea. It was totally bare. In a few places it looked as though it had even been scraped or sandblasted clean.

That thought reminded Blade of the Watchers. He was beginning to wonder if they had ever existed, except in the legends of the village people. Here he was *on top* of the Wall, and he still seemed to be completely invisible to whomever or whatever might be on guard. He was also perfectly happy with this situation.

As Twana's head appeared over the edge, Blade caught another flash of the sun on polished metal. This one was far to the south and came and went so quickly that he wasn't completely sure he hadn't imagined it. He reached down and helped Twana up onto the level surface. She lay gasping for a moment, then rose to her knees and reached for her water bottle. As she drank, Blade again scanned the top of the Wall in both directions, as far as he could see.

Whatever had made the flash was now invisible again. A Watcher? A large metal machine such as Twana had described could make the kind of flashes he'd seen when the sun caught it at the right angle. *If* the Watchers existed, that is—and if they existed, then *where were they?*

Blade and Twana moved swiftly north along the smooth top of the Wall. They went barefoot to reduce noise and leave no visible traces. They kept just far enough away from the edge of the Wall to be invisible from the ground without wandering into the blindness field. If the Watchers no longer mounted a reliable guard on the Wall, the Shoba's men might also discover this. Then they might be willing to climb the hills, and the chase would be on again.

Blade decided that he and Twana would stay up on the Wall for two days, moving as far as they could in that time. That should leave the Shoba's men far behind. With the enemy off their trail, they could return directly to Hores. Blade was no longer quite sure what he'd be doing after that. This Dimension was developing more than the usual quota of mysteries. The Wall seemed to be only a starting point.

They'd been walking for two hours when Blade saw metal flash again, three times in five minutes. The flashes were a good ten miles away, but this time they were to the north. He stopped and desperately strained his eyes to see what might be waiting for them but saw nothing—not even a hint of movement.

After a few minutes they moved on. Blade no longer felt quite so willing to believe that the Watchers were a myth. It occurred to him that they might be playing games with him, like a cat with a mouse, waiting for their chosen moment to strike.

They walked along the Wall all through the rest of the morning and into the afternoon. Every hour or so Blade went down on his belly and crept to the edge of the Wall to examine the plain below. The Shoba's men were nowhere in sight.

Blade decided that, if their pursuers were still out of sight the next morning, he and Twana would climb down from the Wall and take to the ground again. It would be a gamble, but he was beginning to feel it would be less of a gamble than staying on the Wall. Blade had almost a wild animal's instinct for detecting danger, and that instinct was now sending him a clear message. They told him that the Wall was protected— by Watchers or by *something* that was waiting, invisible for the moment, but able to turn deadly dangerous in the blink of an eye.

Midafternoon now, and the sky was growing cloudy. There would be no more reflected sunlight to give warning of whatever might be lying in wait for them, at least not today. Before long the sky had turned gray, and a premature twilight began to spread across the land. Blade and Twana stopped, drank without eating, and went on. Fatigue and strain had bleached Twana's face to the color of bone, and her feet were swollen and blistered. Yet she still seemed quite ready to follow Blade to the end of the Wall, or even farther.

Suddenly Blade heard a faint hooting, like the sound of a distant owl. It came from ahead, but a moment later it was echoed from behind them. Blade stopped and drew his sword. Twana pressed herself against him for a moment, then stepped back, drawing her own sword and standing to guard his back.

The hooting came again, from both in front and behind. It was either louder or closer or both. Then it came a third time. The cat had finished watching the mouse. Now it was stalking. In another moment it would leap. Blade was not sure exactly what the cat would be, but he suspected it would be something against which a sword would be as useless as a feather duster.

The hooting came again, still louder, with a distinct metallic note in it. No living throat could be making that sound. Blade sidestepped toward the edge of the Wall. With only a minute or two more, he could let down the rope to make an escape route for Twana. He himself would probably have to. . . .

Then the hooting was echoed from close at hand, so loudly that the Wall seemed to quiver from the sound. There was a rushing and roaring of violently disturbed air from beyond the blindness field. A blast of wind hit Blade and Twana, hard enough to force the girl to her knees. Something that seemed to be the size of a small house shot high into the air from inside the Wall. It hung in the air above Blade, long enough to give him a grisly moment's anticipation of being crushed flat under it. Then, with another hurricane blast of

58

air and a ringing metallic crash, it came down on top of the Wall.

Twana's mouth fell open, and she gave a gurgling scream of sheer terror. "A Watcher!" she cried. Her sword was shaking in her hand, but somehow she held her ground.

Blade's mouth was open in surprise rather than fear, although he didn't blame Twana. He stared at the Watcher, and from what he had to call its head, two yellowish eyes stared back at him.

The rest of the Watcher—well, start with a rectangular metal box the size of a small truck, set on end. Put the dome-shaped head on top of that, with the eyes, half a dozen antennae, and the twin glassy-blue muzzles of what looked very much like lasers or guns. On each side of the box, stick two arms—the upper one a pair of long, jointed rods ending in massive steel claws, the lower one an eight-foot steel tentacle. Mount the whole thing on a circular base ten feet in diameter. Color it a dirty bronze-tinted blue all over, and add a few dents, patches, and scars.

That was a Watcher, as Richard Blade faced one for the first time on top of the Wall.

He could hear Twana's breath coming in quick gasps, and he didn't blame her. Even if one hadn't gone in fear of the Watchers all one's life, they weren't a pleasant thing to meet. Particularly when there wasn't much hope of either fighting or running.

Those weren't the only choices, fortunately. This machine had to be the creation of an advanced civilization. If its masters were watching through its eyes and listening through its ears, perhaps there was a way to communicate with them. Certainly it was worth trying.

Carefully Blade laid down his sword. Then he straightened up, holding his empty hands well out from his sides, fingers spread wide. If the Watcher's masters were humanoid, the gesture should have its almost universal meaning of "Peace." Then he whispered sharply to Twana, "Do the same as I've done."

"Blade, I—"

"Do it!"

He heard Twana suck in her breath with a hiss. Then at

59

last her courage deserted her, and she turned and ran. Before she'd taken two steps, the Watcher let out another ear-splitting hoot, rose a foot off the ground with a whine and a blast of air, and started after her. All four arms were raised, and both eyes were blinking rapidly.

Blade threw himself to one side, just in time to save his life. A beam of dazzling white light flared from one of the blue muzzles in the Watcher's head. It played across Blade's sword, and when it passed on, it left the metal blackened and warped.

As Blade sprang to his feet, the Watcher's arms on the side toward him lashed out. The tentacle whipped around his knees, while the claw on the upper arm unfolded until it could span his waist. Blade was jerked off his feet and into the air, as the Watcher swept by in pursuit of Twana.

The girl screamed as she saw the Watcher gaining on her. Then she stumbled and went down, the sword flying out of her hand. Blade's arms were free. He reached down to the jointed arm that held him by the waist, grabbed the elbow with both hands, and heaved with all his strength.

It should have been impossible, flesh matched against metal in this way, but Blade's strength somehow made it possible. The arm gave with a screech of twisted and torn metal and went limp, pouring out smoke and sticky bluish fluid. Blade found himself dangling in midair, held only by the tentacle around his knees. He tried to swing himself toward the body of the Watcher. If he could get a firm grip there and then start on the joints with the knife from his belt—

He never made it. The head turned toward him, and Blade had a moment of staring into the mouth of one of the blue tubes—a moment just long enough for him to know that he was about to die.

Then Twana screamed again, and the world dissolved around Blade in white fire and terrible pain.

Chapter 9

Blade awoke in a comfortable bed. He was surprised not only at the bed, but at still being alive to wake up at all. Apparently the Watcher had merely knocked him unconscious, rather than frying him like a piece of bacon. It had left a few traces behind—his head ached, and his skin prickled as if he'd been slightly sunburned all over. He started to sit up, felt a wave of nausea rising in him, and lay down again with his eyes closed until it passed.

At last he sat up and looked around the room. It was impressively large—it would have held all five rooms of his London flat with plenty of space left over. A ceiling of metal hexagons was at least thirty feet above his head. The bed under him was large enough for three or four people and almost too soft for comfort. Red and gray-checked blankets of some musty-smelling synthetic material were piled thickly on it. Blade threw off the blankets and climbed out of the bed.

The floor underfoot was soft and springy, except in a few places where bare stone showed through. The floor covering seemed to grow out of the stone, like pale blue grass, rather than lying on it like a rug.

Apart from the bed, there was nothing in the room but three chairs around a low table in one corner and a large double wardrobe standing in another corner. Blade somehow had the feeling that this austerity was the result of neglect rather than a deliberate decorating scheme.

Except for the wardrobe, the room and everything in it were well-worn, almost shabby. It was absolutely immaculate, as though it were dusted several times a day. But the metal of the ceiling was tarnished, the walls were stained and patched

61

in several places, and the furniture was threadbare and faded. It reminded Blade of the kind of room he'd seen in old houses owned by families who could no longer really afford them, filled with slowly decaying family heirlooms. He wasn't quite sure what he'd expected to find beyond the Wall, but this room certainly wasn't it. If he were supposed to be a prisoner, it was about the oddest cell he'd ever seen!

Blade walked over to the wardrobe. It looked brand-new and was made of something like pale gray plastic with a pebbled finish. When he was three feet away, the front of the wardrobe quietly folded itself up. Inside he saw his clothing and gear, all of it cleaned and hung on hooks as neatly as a trained valet could have done. A quick examination told Blade that nothing was missing except his bow and arrows. Even the knife and the spare sword he'd tied to his pack were there.

He began to wonder if he were a prisoner at all, or some sort of guest. He decided the only way to find out was to search out his captors—or hosts. He also wanted to find Twana. If the Wall-people hadn't killed him, they probably hadn't killed her, but she might be half out of her wits with fear over actually being in the hands of the Watchers. He wanted to calm her, and when he'd calmed her, they could start planning what to do next—including escaping, if that turned out to be necessary.

On the opposite side of the room from the bed was a pointed archway fifteen feet high and ten feet wide. Blade could see a lighted corridor beyond it. He pulled on his clothes and hid the knife in one boot, but left his sword behind. The sword was more likely to offend the Wall-people than protect him from their weapons.

Blade was almost to the archway when there was a sudden metallic rattling and squealing, and another robot entered the room. This one was about the same shape as the Watcher, but lay on its side instead of standing erect. It had eight wheels instead of an air-cushion fan and no visible arms or weapons. Instead, it had large hatches at either end, and in the middle, what looked like a control panel, with knobs, dials, and winking lights.

The robot seemed to detect Blade the moment it entered

the room. It rolled rapidly toward him, then stopped with a last squeal of wheels, so close that he could reach out and touch it. Like the Watcher, this robot showed tarnishing, pitting, and dents that suggested hard use and poor maintenance over many years.

As the robot stopped, the hatch at one end sprang open, and a platform rose up out of the robot's interior. On the platform was a tray holding two metal bottles, several covered dishes, tableware, and a pile of napkins. Room service had arrived without even being called!

The logical thing to do with this free meal was to eat it. Blade did so. The bottles contained water and something tasting vaguely like stale beer. He didn't drink much of it. The food was a vegetable soup, cutlets grained like meat but tasting more like tuna fish, more vegetables so heavily salted they all tasted the same, and a sort of custard pie. Blade had eaten better meals, but not usually in prison. He could eat this food for months if he had to.

He finished the meal and was putting the tray back on the platform when the robot suddenly spoke.

"Was it pleasing to the Master?"

The words came out in a dull, heavy, metallic tone. There was so much crackling and buzzing along with it that it was like listening to a radio during a thunderstorm.

Blade replied, speaking as slowly and distinctly as the robot.

"It was good."

"It is good that the Master is pleased." The robot started to back away. A thought struck Blade.

"Do you wish to please the Master again?"

"It is an order, to please the Master."

"Good. Tell me where the—the woman Master who came with me lives."

The robot sputtered and hissed for so long that Blade thought perhaps he'd asked a question it could not answer. Then the robot's other hatch opened, and what looked like a thin television screen unfolded. A moment later the screen lit up, showing what appeared to be a map of the interior of a building. The robot made a spitting sound, and a sheet of what looked like plastic-coated paper shot out from the top of the screen and fell to the floor.

Blade picked it up. One room was outlined in green, another in red. The robot spoke before he could ask.

"The Master is in the green room. The other Master is in the red room. Is it the Master's wish that they be together?"

Blade was about to say yes, then realized that might make the robot bring Twana to him. He would rather go to her and explore this building on the way.

"The Master will go to the other Master," he said. "That will please both of us." The robot made another spitting sound and produced another map. This one had a route from Blade's room to Twana's, marked out with a silver line that seemed to glow faintly. Blade picked up the second map. "This is good. You have pleased us. You may go." The robot turned about and rolled out of the room.

Spacious living quarters, good food, and now a map that showed him the way to Twana. The mystery of where he was and who had brought him there was growing with every minute. However, finding Twana was still the first thing to do. Blade decided it would be safe to take his sword, took it out of the wardrobe, belted it on, and strode out into the corridor.

The map took him down the corridor, around three successive right-angled turns, then up two flights of stairs. At the second turn Blade found a bathroom, with four large sunken tubs, seven shower stalls, a number of toilets, and two robots watching over it all. The robots were wheeled cones, with four jointed arms at the top and four more spaced equally around the base.

The map now led Blade through a narrow corridor with an arched ceiling and a floor that sloped gently upward. The corridor began to curve around to the left. Blade followed it and abruptly found himself facing one of the armed Watcher robots. In the narrow corridor it looked even bigger and uglier than it had out on the Wall.

The head swiveled toward Blade as the Watcher sensed his presence. He stood where he was, but made no move to disarm himself. The Watcher's reaction should tell him more about whether he was a prisoner or a guest.

The man and the robot stared at each other for several minutes. Each minute seemed like half an hour to Blade. When he was satisfied that the Watcher wasn't simply going to shoot him on the spot, he lowered a hand to the hilt of his sword. Slowly, an inch at a time, he drew the weapon. Then, even more slowly, he raised it to striking position. He was totally alert and ready to drop it if the Watcher showed any reaction at all.

In another minute or two the robot's head began to swivel away from Blade. He let out all the breath he'd been holding and quickly thrust his sword back into the scabbard.

Instantly the Watcher hooted in alarm, and the head swung back toward him, eyes pulsing angrily. Blade froze, with the knowledge that he'd brought himself very close to being killed or stunned. *How*?

Again man and robot faced each other, and again the robot finally turned its head away. Blade's arms flopped to his side almost of their own weight—and again the Watcher went on the alert. This time it raised all four of its arms and held them out toward Blade. Again Blade did his best to imitate a statue for several hour-long minutes. As he stood, his mind was working furiously.

What had alerted the Watcher? Sheathing his sword and dropping his arms to his sides. Both were *movements*. What else did they have in common? Another moment of furious thinking, then. . . .

He'd made both movements *quickly*. Everything else he'd done *slowly*. Could that be it? Could the Watcher be programmed to react to fast movements and ignore slow ones?

It made sense. The Watchers might be programmed to deal with primitive people, who would be frightened by them and run in panic, like Twana. More civilized people, like the Watchers' Masters, would not be frightened. They would not run.

At least it was worth an experiment.

Without waiting for the robot to turn its head away, Blade raised his arms above his head—slowly. Then he lowered them to his sides, even more slowly. The Watcher kept its eyes on him, but was silent. Blade drew his sword, held it over his head for a moment, then slowly sheathed it. By the

65

time he was half done, the Watcher was turning its head away again.

Blade was almost tempted to leave well enough alone, but there was one more thing he felt he had to know. Even more slowly than before he drew his sword. He held it out in front of him and moved toward the Watcher one step at a time. It showed no more response to him than if he'd been ten miles away. He stepped up to it, raised the sword, and laid the edge against the metal body. Nothing happened—nothing at all.

Blade virtually held his breath as he slipped around the robot, sword still held ready to strike. If something did go wrong now, he was fairly sure he could drive the point into the robot's head, taking out its eyes and weapons before it could strike him down.

At last he was past the Watcher and into a stretch of corridor with four doors opening off it, three on the right and one on the left. According to the map, the middle door on the right was Twana's room.

A moment later the map was confirmed. With a shriek that mixed surprise, fear, and delight, Twana burst out of the room into the corridor. She was bare to the waist, and her hair was a tangled mess.

Behind Blade, the Watcher hooted sharply, and a shrill whine filled the corridor as its fan started up. Blade froze and shouted to Twana.

"Stop! Don't move!"

The sheer volume of his voice caught Twana and held her. Behind Blade the whine and hooting of the approaching Watcher grew deafening. He forced himself to take one slow step at a time, as he moved out of the robot's path. If his guess about its programming were correct. . . .

He'd guessed right. The Watcher was already slowing down by the time it passed Blade. Its head was turned toward him, and the arms on one side swept within inches of his face. The Watcher glided slowly up to Twana, looped a tentacle gently over one bare shoulder, then cut off its fan, and settled to the floor with a thud. Twana's eyes were enormous, but she was standing totally motionless. Blade could only hope she wouldn't faint right in front of the Watcher.

She didn't. She stood not even breathing deeply, until the

Watcher drew back its tentacle. Then it glided off the way it had come, to take up its guard post again. Before Twana could faint, Blade scooped her up in his arms and carried her into her room, out of the Watcher's sight. They fell down together on the bed, with Twana's hands pulling at Blade's hair and his lips on her breasts. Somehow they found themselves naked, then locked together in a furious, exuberant joining that held more sheer relief than real desire.

At last they lay together on the bed, catching their breath. Twana raised her head from Blade's chest and drew back her hand from his cheek.

"Blade—*what* were you doing—out there, when you told me to stop? The Watcher could have killed us!"

Blade ran a hand lightly down her back. "You just demonstrated what I think is going to be our best way of getting out of here. I think the Watchers only attack people who are moving fast. You remember that when you stopped, the Watcher slowed down. When you let it touch you without trying to run, it lost interest in you. It didn't think you were dangerous."

"Then—we can go back over the Wall?"

"Perhaps." He didn't want to arouse hopes that might be disappointed, not when there was so much more he needed to find out here. "Certainly we know how to be safe from the Watchers as long as we are here. Meanwhile, we have food, we have water, we have comfortable places to sleep. Are you in such a hurry to leave?"

Twana giggled. "No, I will be happy to stay here for many days." Her lips moved down his body.

Chapter 10

After the next day, Blade knew that he was absolutely right about the Watchers. As long as he moved no faster than a slow walk and made no other quick movements, they would ignore him as if he were no more than a buzzing insect. It would be slow and tedious exploring the whole land here behind the Wall at a snail's pace. It would have been much worse to be trapped in his room by the Watchers until Lord Leighton's computer drew him back to Home Dimension. As long as he moved slowly enough not to alert the Watchers, Blade could go anywhere he pleased. The other robots ignored him completely, no matter how he moved or what he did.

There were several kinds of unarmed work robots. There were the box-like ones that served the meals and did the cleaning. Blade called them Housemaids. There were the Mechanics—the cone-shaped ones he'd seen in the bathroom, who seemed to make all the major repairs. Finally, there were the Gardeners—Mechanics equipped with three extralong telescoping arms that worked in the gardens spreading all around the building where Blade and Twana were staying.

The building itself was a perfect cube of the same bluegray material as the Wall, two hundred feet on a side. From the roof Blade could get a tantalizing view of the land beyond the Wall.

The land rose gently upward for three miles toward the east, to the Wall itself. Most of the distance between the building and the Wall was heavily forested. The trees seemed to form a belt along the Wall, reaching as far as Blade could see. Around the building itself was a stretch of formal gardens, an intricate patchwork of hedges, flowerbeds, gravel paths, streams, and ornamental bridges. Miles away in either direction, Blade could see other cubical buildings, apparently identical to the one he was in.

Toward the west lay more gardens, less carefully tended. In places the grass of the lawns rose knee-high. In other places fallen trees drifted about in the ponds. Blade found only a handful of robots at work here, and those Gardeners were more battered and much slower in their movements than the work robots elsewhere.

So far away to the west that it was visible only from the top of the building lay what looked like a city. By straining his eyes at sunset, Blade could make out the dim silhouettes of high towers. Occasionally he would catch a flash of color, fleeting and mysterious like the flashes of the Watchers on the Wall.

This Dimension seemed to be piling one mystery on top of another, and being beyond the Wall only seemed to be making things worse. There were a hundred and one questions to answer, starting with: Where were the people? Blade could spend half an hour listing them.

One thing seemed reasonably certain. This was a land fast declining. There was an air of shabbiness, neglect, and decay about everything Blade could see. The work robots might be fighting a valiant rearguard action against the ravages of time and weather and plant life, but they were losing.

The best place to start looking for answers seemed to be that city to the west—if it were a city. If it weren't, he could look elsewhere. The only alternative seemed to be wandering aimlessly about in endless miles of forest and garden and perhaps running into defenses that weren't so easily fooled as the Watchers.

Now all that remained was to pick a time and a route for their escape. The Watchers seemed to ignore him no matter how much he was carrying, as long as he moved slowly. If they went on doing this, the escape should be easy.

The escape was even easier than Blade would have dared hope, thanks to the weather.

Whatever forces strengthened the Wall and raised the

blindness field did nothing to fend off the weather. Blade
awoke one night with a chill breeze blowing through the
room from the small window that pierced the outer wall.
Blade unwound himself from the sleeping Twana and went to
the window. As he reached it, the darkness outside exploded
in a raw, white glaze of lightning. Thunder cracked, making
the whole building jump; then as the rumbling died away,
Blade heard the swelling hiss of wind-driven rain. He sprang
back into the room as the first cold drops whipped in through
the window.

Twana sat up in the bed, drawing the blankets around her
shoulders against the breeze. "Put your clothes on," said
Blade. "We're getting out of here. The storm will hide us and
cover our tracks once we're out of the building." Twana
nodded without a word and leaped out of bed.

They pulled on their clothes and picked up their gear and
weapons. Meanwhile, the storm outside was mounting steadily. Rain blew in through the window almost continuously,
soaking the rug.

The Watcher that guarded the corridor was in its usual
place, but getting past it was now routine, even for Twana.
They filled their water bottles in the bathroom and continued
downward. A last flight of stairs, and then a long ramp led
them down to the high-vaulted entrance hall on the ground
floor.

There were more robots in the hall than Blade had ever
seen in one place, including a dozen Gardeners and five
Watchers. He couldn't be sure whether they were on the alert
for emergency work on the building or just getting in out of
the storm. All he could do was move *very* slowly, one cautious step at a time, and keep his hands at his sides.

As stiffly as if they'd been robots themselves, Blade and
Twana made their way through the crowd toward the entrance. Once Blade had to quickly sidestep a Housemaid that
was about to run into him. The nearest Watcher turned its
head to look at him and raised one tentacle, but didn't turn
on its fan or sound the alarm. Blade stood still for a moment,
the Watcher turned away, and he went on.

At last they reached the entrance. By now the wind was
blowing a full gale, and the rain was hitting like blasts from a

71

shotgun. It was as black as the inside of a coal mine, and the wind and the thunder together made a roar that would have drowned out a full-scale battle. There'd never be a better chance to get beyond reach of the robots.

Blade found his feet itching a break into a run. He held back, as a Watcher came wobbling in out of the storm, making slow headway against the wind. With one pair of arms, it was towing a Gardener that had apparently been struck by some heavy falling object. Blade waited until the two robots joined the crowd. Then he took Twana's hand and led her out into the storm.

Instantly the wind gripped them, and the rain lashed at them, driving them along like stampeding cattle. Even when they bent almost double, the pressure of the wind forced them to trot. They didn't even try moving against the wind.

Several times savage gusts almost tore Twana's hand out of Blade's grip. After the fourth gust, Blade led her into the lee of some solid trees and pulled the rope out of his pack. He tied one end of it around Twana's waist and the other around his own. Getting separated, disoriented, and totally lost in this howling darkness were real dangers.

As Blade finished tying the last knot, something fell almost at his feet with a crash like an artillery shell. It was a branch—or rather, the whole top of a tree, with half a dozen branches, each as long as a man and as thick as a man's leg.

With this sort of debris blowing about, it didn't matter how fast he and Twana moved. As long as the storm lasted, the Watchers would be seeing a hundred and one things moving fast enough to alert them. They'd hardly be able to track and examine each one of them. There simply weren't enough Watchers.

A weakness? Yes, but not against the primitive opponents the Watchers were designed to meet. Assuming any primitive opponents got this far beyond the Wall, they wouldn't be out and about tonight. They'd be cowering under cover where they could do no harm.

Richard Blade was not a primitive opponent, even for the most advanced technology.

He led Twana back out into the storm, and after that he let it blow them more or less where it would. It would be

72

easier to make up lost ground when the storm died than try to fight it while it was blowing, and they _had_ to get as far as they could before the robots realized they were gone.

So the storm blew them onward. It blew them across a bridge and nearly blew them into the stream under the bridge. They entered the trees again on the other side of the stream and passed down a long, narrow path. The trees on either side looked like pines and stood eighty or a hundred feet tall, but they were bending like blades of grass in the storm. The path was already littered with fallen branches, and more were crashing down every minute.

They came out of the trees onto the shore of a small lake. It was only a few acres, but the storm was whipping up respectable waves. The water was churning ankle-deep over the stepping stones they used to cross the lake. Once Twana slipped and went to her knees in the water, but Blade pulled her to her feet and half-carried her the rest of the way across.

They moved on, listening to the roar of the wind and the thunder, the crackle and crash of falling trees, the hammering beat of the rain, until they were half-deaf. They were thoroughly drenched, and Blade was beginning to wonder if he were losing his sense of direction. He kept on though—it would be safer to get completely lost than to arouse the suspicion of the robots.

How long he and Twana kept going it was impossible to guess. Blade only knew that it was still pitch dark and blowing a gale when Twana began to stumble and stagger. She shook her head and mouthed the words, "I can't go on." Blade lifted her onto his back, with her arms clamped about his neck.

His own legs were beginning to ache and stiffen when they finally reached something that could serve as shelter. It was a small stone house, open on one side. Fortunately, the open side faced away from the storm, so the interior was reasonably dry. Blade carried Twana inside and set her down in a corner. He would have liked to make a fire, but there was nothing to burn, nothing to light it with, and too much risk of being spotted by the robots.

Inside, Blade and Twana stripped, wrapped themselves in their soggy blankets, and lay down to get as much sleep as

73

they could. Exhaustion quickly sent them off to sleep, with the storm still howling in their ears.

In the morning the storm was still blowing as hard as ever, and Twana flatly refused to face it again. Blade began to wonder if he'd have done better to leave her in the building by the Wall and do his exploring on his own. Twana could cope with the robots, and they would probably protect her from any other danger until he returned.

However, he and Twana were both committed now, and something good might come of her joining him. The more she saw with her own eyes about what lay beyond the Wall, the more she could tell her own people, and the more likely they were to believe her. Blade was sure that knowing more about what lay beyond the Wall would help the villagers. If it did nothing else, it would ease their supersitious fear of the Watchers.

By late afternoon the wind was no more than a stiff breeze, and the clouds were breaking up. Blade saw several Gardener robots pass the house, most of them carrying fallen branches in their claws. He and Twana headed straight west until darkness overtook them, seeing a good many more Gardeners, but only one Watcher. They passed it slowly, and it ignored them as if they were only leaves blown on the wind. There didn't seem to be any hunt on for them yet.

They slept that night on the driest patch of ground they could find, deep inside a pine grove. When morning came, Blade scrambled up to the top of the tallest tree he could find and took his bearings. They'd come far enough so that in the pale morning light he could make out hints of the distant city from this lower perch. It looked as if they still had a long walk ahead of them, so the sooner they got started, the better.

They had to walk all that day and most of the next. Every hour or so Blade climbed a tree to check direction. The city was always there, though for a long time it seemed to be getting no closer. At times during the first day, Blade almost suspected the city was a phantom, receding into the distance, as he and Twana advanced toward where they thought it was.

Toward evening he could see the sunset light flashing from

dozens of ranked metal towers. The city was there. What surprised him was realizing its size. It must be a good ten of fifteen miles wide, and many of those towers had to be at least
a mile high. Blade was tempted to push on through the
darkness but decided against it. What lay around him was no
longer any sort of garden, but rank wilderness that might
hold all sorts of surprises.

This area might have been a garden once. Twice Blade saw
heavily overgrown patches of tumbled stone, once the remains of a bridge. But here the neglect that was overtaking
the land closer to the Wall had gone totally unchecked for
many years. Even the robots seemed to shun this land. Blade
hadn't seen one all afternoon.

They pushed on at dawn the next day. For the first few
hours they faced a tangle of vegetation that would have done
justice to a tropical jungle. Blade would gladly have traded
one of their swords for a machete.

Then abruptly they came out into open country, rolling
away toward the city that was now clearly visible from the
ground for the first time. Somehow, in spite of its size and
the hundred or more shimmering towers, the city looked ster-
ile and asleep, even dead. It seemed to radiate a vast, overpowering silence that spread across the country and
swallowed up even the sigh of the wind and the crunch of
Blade's and Twana's footsteps through the brittle grass.

Blade wondered for a moment if he'd taken off on a wild-
goose chase after a dead city. Still, there was no point in calling the city a corpse until he'd at least tried to take its pulse!
He lengthened his stride.

They covered the last miles to the city in a couple of
hours. As they drew closer, Blade saw the city had its own
wall. It was the same height as the Wall outside, but this one
was studded with featureless cylindrical towers about every
hundred yards. Towers and wall both seemed to be made of
something that looked like frosted, white glass. There was no
shimmering in the air over his wall and no glint of metal
from prowling Watchers. This wall looked as dead as the city
behind it.

The wall stood unbroken as far as Blade could see, but
once more the storm had been his friend. A good many trees

grew along the wall, and one of them had fallen against it. Branches large enough to support a man jutted almost up to the top of the wall. Blade and Twana headed toward the tree.

Blade dropped his pack and other gear and scrambled up the tree. Some of the branches sagged under his weight, but all of them held. In a few minutes he crawled out onto the top of the city wall. On hands and knees he crept toward the inner side of the wall, half-expecting to stick his head into yet another weird energy field.

Instead, he found himself staring down at the ground. The city wall was barely ten feet thick. At the foot of the wall was a belt of what looked like faded green concrete. Beyond it was another stretch of ragged garden. Two miles away the buildings of the city began, mounting up like a mountain range, from five-story foothills to the crowning peaks of the mile-high towers. Nothing moved except the grass, where it was long enough to ripple in the wind.

Blade sighed. It looked as if he *had* come all this way to reach a dead city.

He crawled back across the wall, threw one end of the rope down, and saw Twana tie his gear and weapons to it. He pulled them up, put on his sword belt, then threw the rope down again. A moment later Twana was standing beside him.

In the moment after that, the city came horribly alive. The nearest tower, fifty yards away, sprouted lean, red-clad figures with gleaming blue rifles in their hands. "Get down!" Blade shouted, grabbing Twana's belt as he dropped flat.

He was seconds too slow. One of the figures raised his rifle, sighted, and fired. Air crackled and blurred, and a halo of white danced around Twana's head. She gave a choked cry and threw her arms out wildly to keep her balance. She took a drunken, reeling step; then one flailing foot came down on the empty air inside the wall. She vanished with a scream that ended in a crunch as she struck the ground fifty feet below.

Then there was silence—except for the sharp hiss of Blade's indrawn breath as he stood up and the softer hiss of steel as he drew his sword.

Chapter 11

Blade had enough self-control left not to charge or even shout. He stood where he was, staring at the cluster of red figures on the tower. He stared as if the intensity of his stare could draw them down from their perch and into range of his sword.

A part of his mind told him that he shouldn't do this, that he was endangering himself and his chances of peaceful realtions with the people of this city. It was only a small part of his mind that said this, and the rage in Blade made him totally deaf to it. He didn't care about the danger to himself, not if he could take a few of those red-suited sharpshooters with him. As for peaceful relations—as far as he could see, these people couldn't have cared less about that. If they were going to be this trigger-happy. . . .

Or were they? There seemed to be confusion among the men on the tower. Two of them seemed to be arguing with the man who'd fired. The wind blurred the words past understanding, but they all seemed to be thoroughly excited about something. Their lean bodies were taut, and their arms waved about frantically. It looked as though something unexpected had happened. Could it be Twana's death—if she were dead? Blade risked stepping over to the edge of the wall and looking down. After a moment he looked away. Even from up here he could tell that he'd brought Twana to her death. She lay face down, her head twisted at an angle to her body that nothing living could ever take.

As Blade stepped back from the edge of the wall, the soldiers started disappearing from the top of the tower. A moment later a door opened onto the top of the wall, dilating like the lens of a camera. Five soldiers filed out and came toward Blade. All of them were carrying their rifles at the ready. The one who'd fired trailed a little behind the other four, and Blade saw the others looking uncertainly back at him. Blade relaxed slightly, but did not sheath his sword and went on willing the soldiers to come closer. If they kept on, they'd be so close that they could hardly use their rifles without hitting each other. He would have no such problem with his sword.

The soldiers came on. Their boots, coveralls, and helmets were all fire-engine red. Apparently they'd never heard of camouflage, or else had no need of it. Their rifles were streamlined, with silver barrels and stocks and butts of dark-blue plastic. They carried black truncheons and small cylindrical green boxes on their web belts. The faces under the helmets. . . .

The faces had human shape and human features, but all five sets of features were as identical as so many stamped coins. The skin of their faces and hands flexed and creased like living skin, but it had a waxy sheen that Blade had never seen, except in the skin of a dying man or a corpse.

More robots. No, not robots—androids. Artificial beings in human shape, perhaps organic, perhaps with all the parts and processes of a human being. Nonetheless, artificial creations of a biological science generations beyond that of Home Dimension. Were they programmed like the robots, or had they been given human intelligence to match their human forms? Certainly their greater physical versatility would make them more formidable opponents than the Watchers.

Blade decided to take the initiative and see what came of it. As the androids approached, he raised his sword and held in out in front of him, barring the androids' path.

"Halt! What is your business here?"

The five androids stopped as if they'd run into a stone wall, and the one who'd fired raised his rifle to his shoulder. One of his comrades grabbed it by the barrel and, with an angry growl, drew it down again. "He commands like a Master, (a meaningless gabble that might have been a name or a number)," the restraining android said sharply.

"He is not a Master," said the other.

"We do not know that."

"Ask him, then," said a third android. All of them spoke without changing the expressionless blankness of their faces. They all spoke in a clipped, almost comically precise fashion, biting off their words so quickly that Blade had to listen carefully to understand what they were saying.

"You need not ask," he said. "I am a Master."

"You are not of the Authority," said the one who'd fired. He did not raise his rifle, but now his voice held a distinct note of anger that Blade didn't like. "No Master who is not of Authority leaves the Houses of Peace."

"I am of the Authority," said Blade. "I have been ordered to travel beyond the wall of the city. The Master you killed was with me. The Authority will not be pleased at what you have done."

This had no effect on the hostile android, but the other four looked at each other. Finally one of them said, "We must keep you here and call the Authority. They will tell us who you are."

"You doubt the word of a Master," said Blade. He made it a statement, not a question. He also made his voice flat and cold, deliberately menacing.

"Yes," said the hostile android. The others were silent and seemed to be thoroughly uncomfortable about the whole situation.

"It is not permitted to doubt the word of a Master," said Blade sharply. "Since you have done that which is not permitted, you shall give me your weapon." He shifted his feet slightly apart, into combat stance, and watched the android's hands and eyes. From long experience he knew that dividing one's enemies and setting them against each other was always a step in the right direction.

"I—will—not—give—it!" said the android. Each word was at a higher pitch than the one before it, until the last one came out a shrill scream.

Blade took a step sideways and got ready to drop his sword and close with the hysterical android. Before he could do anything more, the android went into action. The muzzle of its rifle swung toward Blade. Blade started to drop to his knees, ready to go in under the rifle with the sword. Before either the android or Blade could complete their movements, one of the other androids leaped forward. The hysterical android fired by sheer reflex. The white beam of the rifle took the second android in the head at a range of no more than a single foot. His mouth sagged open, his eyes dissolved into pulp, blood gushed from his nose. He went to his knees, dropping his own rifle. One hand clutched at his killer's belt. Then he went forward on his face in a widening pool of silver-tinged blood.

Blade dropped his sword and snatched up the fallen rifle. Before he could bring it into action, another android closed with the killer, grabbing his rifle and shoving the muzzle skyward. The killer held on grimly and tried to back away, dragging his attacker with him. Blade and the last two androids raised their rifles and sighted on the killer. Before they could fire, the killer whirled around, swinging his attacker with him. The other android gave a tremendous heave, pulling his opponent off his feet but going down with him.

The two androids rolled over and over, kicking and clawing at each other, so thoroughly tangled together that Blade and the other androids didn't dare fire. The fighting androids rolled over several more times, reached the edge of the wall, and vanished over it. Unlike Twana, they did not scream. There was a moment of ghastly silence, then a double-barreled thud, and the crackle of one of the rifles fired by dead fingers. The rifle fired until the air reeked of ozone, then died away, leaving silence behind it.

Blade was the first to break the silence. He pointed his rifle at the last two androids and spoke sharply. "You will give me your weapons. You will go into the tower. You will stay there until the Authority gives you an order to leave. You are all *unreliable*." The two androids shuddered at the last word. Blade wondered if it had some special meaning in their programming or training.

"We shall please the Master." The two androids knelt, put down their rifles, and remained kneeling while Blade picked up the weapons. He examined them, found the power sources, and removed them. Each power source was a small red box, about the size of a pocket calculator. Blade put both boxes in his pack, then hammered the rifles on the top of the wall until they broke apart.

"Now I shall go down from the wall and go to the Authority," he said. The androids nodded. Still kneeling, one of them touched the top of the green cylinder of his belt. Blade heard a faint hiss and saw a ladder reaching all the way to the ground slide out from the inner face of the wall.

"I am pleased," he said. "You may now go to your tower." Blade waited until the androids had vanished, then scrambled down the ladder.

The two fallen androids were both as dead as Twana. Blade left them lying where they'd fallen but took the power cells of their rifles. Then he lifted Twana's body on his back and carried it a mile toward the city. Inside a circle of close-grown trees, he used the girl's own sword to dig a grave. When the grave was deep enough, he laid Twana in it, with her weapons beside her. Then he pushed the earth back over her and finally piled heavy stones from a fallen wall on the grave. When he'd finished, he was filthy and sweating, and he suspected he'd taken more time than he should have.

He also knew that he could have done no less. His good intentions had only brought Twana on a long and futile journey to a wretched death and a lonely grave far from her own village and her own people. He could at least give her a decent burial.

Then he washed himself off in the nearest pond, gathered up weapons and pack, and headed toward the city.

Blade followed an intricate path through the gardens, keeping under cover as much as possible. He hoped he'd kept the two androids on the wall from sounding the alarm or setting up ambushes for him, but he didn't trust them. He did not intend to be an easy target for any of the city's defenders—robot, android, human, or anything else.

Apparently there were some living human beings in this city, or at least there had been within the memory of the androids. He'd be more careful and conciliatory in his approach to these humans, if he found them. He'd also have a few things to tell them about their pet android soldiers!

It took Blade several hours to creep to the edge of the city.

By that time it was getting dark, and a rising wind hinted at another storm coming. Blade started looking for an intact, but uninhabited, building to shelter him for the night. Before he entered the city, he stopped and tied one of his spare knives to the muzzle of his rifle with a length of cord. It was an improvised and precarious bayonet, but enough to be a thoroughly unpleasant surprise to any enemy who came to close quarters.

With the rifle held ready, Blade entered the city. It was silent except for the eerie piping of the rising wind, and there was nothing moving—not even a rat or a bird. But this was not a dead city. Shabby, certainly—like the building by the Wall, there were stains and patches and signs of neglect and wear in every street and on every building.

But most of the dark windows held their glass, the tightly closed doors stood straight, the grass of the lawns was neatly clipped, and the streets were swept free of dust and debris. In one street Blade found five six-wheeled trucks parked, and each one was as clean as if it had just come out of a dealer's showroom. They had clear bubble cabs and fat tires that seemed to be made of some sort of woven metal mesh. He could not tell what sort of engine drove them.

There was life in this city—hidden, or perhaps asleep, but certainly there. Blade kept scanning the windows, hoping to surprise some lurking observer. He saw nothing. The streets were bare of cover, and Blade began to feel disagreeably naked and exposed to whatever might be waiting for him.

By now it was almost dark, and he felt a heaviness in the air that told him the storm was close. He came to a ramp leading down to what looked like the mouth of a tunnel and went down into it.

He'd just discovered that the tunnel was barred off by a metal screen, when he heard two sounds. One was the swelling hiss of rain; the other was the unmistakable whine of an engine and the whisper of tires on the street. Blade raced back up the ramp, in time to see one of the six-wheeled trucks roll by. Inside the cab were four figures—one of the android soldiers, two men in blue coveralls, and someone in black with golden hair shining under a green cap. Blade lay flat at the top of the ramp, watching the lights of the truck fade away in the rain.

To his surprise, it stopped no more than a hundred yards down the street. Blade remembered there was an open courtyard with a lawn just about there. Then he dimly saw people climbing out of a cab and flitting about.

At this point the rain started coming down so hard that Blade could no longer see clearly. He smiled, for he'd seen enough. It looked as though some of the people in this city were coming to him, instead of his having to go search them out. He stood up and strode through the rain toward the truck's dim lights.

Chapter 12

Blade was halfway to the lights when they suddenly moved off to the left and out of sight. He crossed the street and used the wall of the building there for cover. He stalked up to the entrance to the courtyard and peered around the edge of the building.

The truck was parked at the inner end of the courtyard. The two men in blue coveralls were unloading cylindrical containers from the back platform. The man in the green cap was standing by a small, glossy white door. The soldier android sat in the driver's seat of the truck, its rifle across its knees.

Hard common sense told Blade to pick off the soldier first, from cover. The hope of good relations with the people of this city, or at least information from them, told him otherwise. He compromised by unslinging the rifle and inserting a fresh power cell. Then with the rifle held ready, he stepped out into the courtyard.

The android was the first to spot Blade and the quickest to act. It leaped to the ground, raising its rifle as it did. Blade didn't let the android complete the movement. His own rifle snapped up, and its beam flared white, reflected from the rain and lighting up the whole courtyard. The android was knocked back against the truck, then slumped to the ground. Blade dashed toward the truck, water spraying from under his boots.

The two laborers dropped their loads, turned and ran. As they passed Blade, he saw that their faces had the same mass-produced appearance and waxy sheen as the soldiers'. So the laborers were androids too! Before Blade could learn any more about them, they dashed out of the courtyard and vanished into the rain.

Blade reached the truck as the man in the green cap flattened himself against the white door and fumbled in a pouch at his belt. Blade held his fire. The man's face had high cheekbones, a fair complexion flushed with excitement, and large, dark eyes that looked at Blade without flinching. This was a human being, not an android. Blade didn't fire; he didn't want to chance the effects of the shock rifle on a human system.

Instead, he stepped out from behind the truck and advanced toward the man. The man jerked a metal rod out of the belt pouch and pressed the larger end against the door. Nothing happened. Desperation flashed across his face. He dropped the rod and jerked something like a short-barreled pistol with an oversized cylindrical butt. Blade dove forward and down as the pistol came up to bear on him. Something went *whee-whee-whee* very rapidly just above his head, and behind him something else went *crannnnng*!

Then he was rolling, coming up under the man's defenses, ready to use the rifle butt to strike a disabling blow. With astounding speed, the man leaped clear over Blade and aimed an expert kick at his exposed back. Blade twisted aside just in time to take the kick on his hip. If it had struck where it had been aimed, it would have cracked his spine.

Blade bounced to his feet and thrust at the man with his bayonet. The man danced aside as expertly as before and raised his pistol. Blade slammed the barrel of his rifle across the man's wrist and saw the gun drop to the ground. He also saw something else. In all the confusion, the man's cap had fallen off, and his hair had come down. It shimmered like raw gold in the light from the truck's cab. Now that he could see the hair, the full face, the outline of the body under the black coverall, Blade realized he was fighting a woman.

He also realized that she was as determined to kill him as any opponent he'd ever met, and probably a good deal more capable of doing so than most.

The woman jumped backward a good three feet and turned to snatch up the android's rifle. She was diving for it when Blade aimed his own rifle at the fallen weapon and fired. His beam triggered off the power cell. There was a *whoooffff*, a shower of white sparks, and a cloud of greasy smoke. The rifle flew apart into two blackened pieces.

The woman somersaulted completely over the destroyed rifle like a trained tumbler and came up as though she had steel springs in her legs. Blade raised his rifle to avoid spitting her on the bayonet as she came in. She detected the movement almost the instant it began. Blade took another jarring kick on his thigh but couldn't fend off a flattened hand slashing painfully into his ribs. He realized that, if he weren't going to shoot the woman, he'd better drop the rifle and get both hands free. He let the weapon fall and grabbed for the woman. His hands closed on empty air as she danced back out of reach, aiming a kick at his kneecap as she retreated.

Her timing was a little off. Blade sidestepped completely and clamped one hand on the woman's leg. The material of her coverall was as slick as glass, and she twisted furiously, breaking Blade's grip. She kicked again, driving Blade back as she went over in another somersault and came up again facing him.

At this point Blade decided he'd better not take any more chances with the woman. She didn't seem to be at all interested in any sort of friendly relations with him. She was also one of the fastest and deadliest opponents he'd ever faced in unarmed combat.

This time when the woman came at him, Blade struck first. He kicked out in the same moment she did, catching her off balance, bringing her down. She was on her feet before he could fall on top of her with his two hundred and ten pounds, but not before he was inside her defenses. She brought her knee up into Blade's groin but not hard enough to cripple him. Blade clamped both arms around her and pulled her against him. She tried to butt him under the chin with her head. He grabbed her hair with one hand, pulling her head back far enough to keep her teeth from his throat. Then he jabbed three fingers of the other hand into the pit of her stomach. It was like jabbing a plate of flexible steel, but for a moment she stopped fighting. He was able to get his hands around her neck and apply his thumbs to the great blood vessels there. At last she went limp. Blade lowered her to the

87

ground, made sure she was still breathing, retrieved the rifle, and stood up again. It was a couple of minutes before he caught his breath and felt entirely steady on his legs.

This hadn't been the best way to introduce himself to the human population of this city. However, what was done was done. The next thing to do was get some clothes that might discourage the soldier androids from shooting at him on sight. Of course! What better disguise than the red coveralls and helmet of one of those same androids!

Blade stripped the dead soldier. Under the coveralls, it wore a reinforced garment covering torso and groin, like an armored vest from Home Dimension. Under the vest, it was naked. Blade was not surprised to see that it had neither navel, breasts, nor any visible sex organs. It didn't even have any body hair, except a sparse growth on the head.

He was able to pull on both the vest and the coverall and still breathe and move comfortable. He put the helmet on his head, tightened the chin strap, and looked at himself in the cab of the truck. The woman's pistol had shattered or cracked half of it, but there was still enough left to give Blade a good image of himself. His complexion was hopelessly wrong, but otherwise he'd do well enough, at least in the darkness. He wasn't going to be roaming about this city by daylight until he'd asked somebody a few pointed questions about the androids and a good many other things!

The next thing to do was to get the woman some place that was out of the rain and where they wouldn't be interrupted or bothered by anyone, human or android. He remembered the rod she'd been tapping against the door. He picked it up and went to work on the door, feeling with one hand and using the rod with the other. At last he felt a circular panel sunk a fraction or an inch into the door. He pressed the rod hard into the center of the panel.

The third time he pressed, the door quivered, then slid gently aside. It was solid metal, nearly a foot thick, and Blade heard faint grating and grinding noises as its immense weight moved. It revealed a long corridor, bathed in pale blue light, with a number of rooms opening off each side. It looked remarkably like one of the corridors in the building by the Wall. Blade pulled on his pack, lifted the woman in his arms, and carried her inside.

As if his appearance had conjured them out of the air, two of the blue-clad worker androids popped out of the nearest doorway. The combination of blue light and blue coveralls made their waxy complexions look even ghastlier than usual. Both of them stopped and looked at Blade, but neither of them said a word. Blade would have given a good deal for those totally expressionless faces to show some emotion he could interpret, but they were as blank as ever.

After a moment one of the androids went over to the doorway and pressed his hand against a plate set in the wall beside it. The door slowly closed behind Blade. In silence he walked down the corridor. The androids stood like a pair of sentries at the end of the corridor until they seemed to realize they weren't going to get any orders from Blade. Then they disappeared back into their room.

The rooms along the corridor were all very much like what Blade had seen in the building by the Wall—large, clean, shabby, and sparsely furnished. In the center of one room, an intricate sculpture of silvery metal spirals stood on a stone pedestal. The metal sculpture was the first really decorative object Blade had seen in this whole Dimension. Somehow that made him feel more at home, so he chose that room.

The woman was still unconscious when Blade laid her down on the bed. Her hair was a sodden mess, but her coverall was as dry as if she'd been taking a walk on a spring morning. The material seemed to be water-repellant to an extraordinary degree.

Blade made no effort to undress the woman. Instead, he propped her head up on several pillows, then tied both her hands and feet as securely as he could without making the knots painfully tight. After that he searched the room.

He learned nothing he hadn't known before, until he came to the wardrobe. This one also opened itself at his approach, revealing a dozen robe-like garments in as many different lengths and colors. Several were nearly transparent, and two looked as though moths had been at them for years. They were more holes than fabric.

Blade took off his helmet and pulled on the largest of the

robes. It concealed the red coverall completely. He look one of the moth-eaten robes, cut it into strips with his knife, and carefully gagged the woman. She might not be able to order the worker androids to fight him, but she could probably order them to call the soldiers or other humans.

Finally, Blade pulled the blankets over the woman until only her head was visible. Then he took his sword and rifle and went out into the corridor. The woman looked as though she'd be quietly unconscious for another couple of hours. That would be plenty of time for him to get around and do a little exploring on his own. He might find a few of the answers he was looking for. That could put him in a stronger position to get the rest of the answers from the woman when she woke up, without having to do anything drastic to her.

Chapter 13

One of the workers was moving down the corridor with a box in its hands as Blade came out of the room. It stopped and said, "What will please the Master?"

It seemed the workers would take him for a Master, now that he had a Master's clothes on. Good. Apparently a Master could go anywhere—unless he ran into a mad soldier—and all he had to do was give orders.

"I wish you to take me to the top of this building," he said. "I will be pleased to walk about in it."

The worker was silent for a moment. Then it said, "That is Physical." The emphasis it placed on the word implied the capital letter.

Blade sensed he'd done something that wasn't part of the android's notions of a Master's behavior. But he wasn't going to sit on his arse simply to keep these damned androids happy!

"I will be pleased to walk about in the building," he repeated. "Your orders are to please the Masters."

The android nodded slowly. "This is a House of Peace. Does the Master wish assistance with the Inward Eye?"

"No, I do not wish assistance. I wish to walk about in the building."

"That is Physical," said the android again.

Blade was tempted to ask why something being Physical was so important but decided against it. That might reveal a degree of ignorance sufficient to make even a worker android suspicious.

He shook his head. "It will not be pleasing to the Master if you do not obey. Is this clearly understood? If you do not take me where I want to go, you will be unreliable."

The last word did the same thing to the worker as it had done to the soldiers on the city wall. The android stiffened and quivered all over. "The Master will be pleased," it said unsteadily.

"Good," said Blade. "Lead the way." He pointed with the rifle. The android turned and headed down the corridor. Blade followed it to the far end and through a low archway. Beyond was a large, square room with a railed, circular metal platform in the middle. The android went over to the platform and beckoned Blade up onto it. He looked up and saw a circular shaft slightly larger than the platform rising up into the darkness above it. Then the android gripped a section of the railing and twisted it. The platform shot straight up from the floor and into the shaft with a faint humming sound.

Blade gripped the railing and watched the walls of the shaft flow past. At intervals they shot through large, square rooms like the one on the ground floor, so fast that it was impossible for Blade to see what was in them. Apparently the android was taking Blade's wish to go up to the top of the building as a literal order.

Several minutes later Blade finally saw the sheen of a metal ceiling above him. It grew rapidly larger, until he could make out patterns of metal ribs. Then the platform soared up out of the shaft, lurched sideways, and thudded down on the floor, nearly knocking Blade off his feet.

Blade stepped off the platform and looked around. His first impression was that he'd wandered into the middle of a high-society orgy. On a low dais piled with rugs and pillows, a couple was making love. A red-haired woman lay naked on a mat on the floor, while an android wearing only blue shorts straddled her buttocks and back, massaging her steadily and expertly. Three other people—two men and a woman—stood chest deep in a large glass tub. Two androids were scrubbing them with sponges on long handles, while a third played a hose over them. Blade caught a heavy scent of perfume from the water.

That was just a start. The room was more than sixty feet on a side and not only clean, but luxuriously furnished and well maintained. There were about forty human beings in it, and more than a hundred androids at work bathing them, massaging them, serving them food and drink, even carrying them about in small sedan chairs of light metal and plastic. It was not an orgy—only one couple was making love—or any sort of party that Blade could imagine.

He sniffed the air carefully for drugs but could detect none. Yet all the people were dull-eyed and languid in their movements, as oblivious to his presence as if he'd been another of the androids. Something certainly had their attention fogged and confused, even if it weren't drugs.

As Blade finished his tour of the room, the redhead who'd been getting the massage turned over and looked at him. She lay with her chin in one hand, obviously trying to decide whether to invite him to join her. Finally, she shook her head. "No," she said in a sleepy voice, "no, I have taken it only through the Inward Eye. It would be too Physical to change the way now." She rolled back over on her stomach and seemed to drift off to sleep.

There was that "Inward Eye" again, whatever it was. Mystery was piling itself on mystery. Apparently the Inward Eye could be a sex substitute, but so could a great many other things. The redhead hadn't told Blade very much!

Then he realized, with a mild shock, that even if the woman had beckoned to him, he wouldn't have gone. Not that she wasn't attractive. In fact, she was breathtakingly beautiful—long-limbed, exquisitely curved, with great green eyes, that flaming head of red hair, full lips, everything she needed.

In fact, she was too beautiful, too perfect. She was like one of those fashion models turned by make-up, diet, and exercise into an Image of Beauty rather than a living woman. Blade had never cared for that sort of woman in Home Dimension, and this woman was even worse.

Blade looked around the room again, and with a further shock realized something he hadn't clearly noticed before. Every woman and every man in the room had that same quality of unnatural beauty, health, and personal perfection. The more clearly he realized this, the less plausible it seemed.

The android who'd escorted him was standing by the platform. Beyond the platform another corridor opened off the

93

room. Blade could see lighted doorways on either side. He headed off down the corridor, determined to explore further.

He found himself moving through an even stranger world than the big room. All the rooms here were also spotlessly clean and beautifully kept, with a decadent display of cushions and tapestries, jewels and polished metal, weird abstract sculptures, and still more weird and abstract paintings, carved and inlaid furniture.

In the center of every room was an enormous bed. About half of these beds were empty, although some had androids busily at work on them. The others were occupied, always by a single person who was apparently sound asleep.

All of these sleepers wore metal mesh helmets on their heads, with solid, heavy bands around their temples. All wore black masks over their eyes. Otherwise they were completely naked.

Beside the bed of each sleeper stood a large, polished, black metal box mounted on four wheels. Wires led from it to the metal helmets. On top were a control panel and a series of slots. Two androids stood beside each box, apparently keeping a close watch on it and on the sleeper.

Although they seemed to be sound asleep, the people in the beds also seemed to be having some rather interesting dreams. Several were kicking furiously or churning their legs in running movements. Blade saw two men with erections and one woman writhing in the grip of orgasm.

At last Blade felt he'd seen enough on this floor. He led the android back to the platform and motioned toward the shaft. The platform lurched into the air, then dropped through the hole in the floor.

Blade examined eight different floors in the building before deciding there was no point in going on. With minor variations, each floor was the same. A large room at one end, with a corridor leading off it. On each floor sixty to a hundred of the private rooms and sixty to a hundred people. About half the people asleep and wired into the black boxes, the other half in the large room being tended by the androids or (very rarely) talking or making love to each other. Always a small army of blue-clad worker androids—at least two for every human being. Always the languid movements and the blank

94

stares, the apathetic manner, and the inhuman perfection of the human bodies.

Blade realized that he had not only seen enough, he couldn't really *stand* seeing any more for the moment. The people of this city seemed to grow more weird and incomprehensible the more he learned about them! They were not dead, but they hardly seemed to be doing much he could call living.

He'd walked into a city of the living dead, and his first impulse was to walk right back out of it again. Still, there was too great a mystery here to leave behind, not to mention too much that might be worth bringing back to Home Dimension.

There might even be a chance to help these people—if they weren't past wanting help, or even realizing that they might need it.

Blade didn't realize until he started back down how long he'd taken in his exploration of the building. Through a window he could see dawn creeping across the city. If the woman hadn't been discovered and released by the workers, she might have suffocated. At the very least, she'd be trying to scream her head off. When the android let him off the platform at the bottom of the shaft, Blade practically sprinted down the corridor to the room where he'd left the woman.

She was still there, alive, and quietly asleep rather than unconscious or hysterical. She'd certainly done her best to get free—her wrists were raw from the chafing of the rope. Seeing that she wasn't going to get free though, she'd settled down to regain her strength.

This woman was formidably cool-headed and competent—dangerously so, if she remained an enemy. It wouldn't be enough just to interrogate her. He'd have to win her over, as a friend or an ally. Otherwise he'd have to kill her outright, keep her a prisoner, or spend the rest of his time in the city of the living dead trying to look in all directions at once. Blade didn't like any of these alternatives.

Blade ordered two of the workers to bring him a meal, for two Masters. When the meal came, he set the woman's tray aside and emptied his own. The food and cooking were superb—better than Blade had eaten in most expensive Home Dimension restaurants. There people obviously had settled their priorities a long time ago. Never mind if the gardens ran to wilderness or the soldiers ran amuck—as long as the baths were hot and the steaks were rare, all was right with the world.

Yet how did this explain the woman he'd taken prisoner, so skilled and deadly that it had nearly been the other way around? She certainly had not achieved her skill through a lifetime of sybaritic self-indulgence and being waited on hand and foot by androids!

Blade looked at the woman and realized that she was awake and looking at him. He smiled. "The androids have brought a meal for you. If I untie you so that you can eat, will you promise not to call out?"

Their eyes met, and she nodded slowly. Blade guessed he could trust her, but decided to make sure. He sent the serving androids out into the corridor, then closed the door and dragged the table and several chairs in front of it. That would delay the woman in getting out or the androids in getting in. Only then did he take off the woman's gag and untie her wrists. He left her ankles bound and sat in a chair between the bed and the door with his rifle across his lap while she ate.

When she'd finished, Blade untied the knife he'd been using as a bayonet. With the knife in his belt, he sat down on the foot of the bed. He had no intention of laying a finger on the woman again, except in self-defense. He was not yet ready to let her know this.

Blade suspected the woman was of the Authority—the government or police of this city. He also suspected that it had been a long time since even the Authority had come face to face with a civilized person from outside the city. Blade was the unknown, and the unknown always had the ability to sow terror or at least uncertainty in the toughest and best-trained people.

"My name is Richard Blade," he began. "I come from England. I have traveled far and entered this city of yours in peace. I have not found—"

The woman frowned and held up a hand. It was a long-fin-

96

gered, graceful hand, in spite of the distinctive calluses from many years of unarmed-combat training. "England. What was it called, when it was a City of Peace?"

"I do not know that our land has ever been called anything but England," said Blade. "Certainly there are no records that give another name."

"You do not even remember that you *were* a City of Peace?"

"As I said, we have nothing left that tells us so." Blade pretended to frown in concentration. "Some say there was once a mighty city called Rome, which ruled all the world and then disappeared. But most among the people of England consider this a tale to amuse children, no more."

The woman shook her head, and her voice held a note of sadness, "It has been a long time since the Cities of Peace ceased to talk to one another. Perhaps it has been long enough even for what you say to have happened. Certainly you are the first to enter Mak'loh from another City in the lifetime of anyone in the Authority, and some of us are no longer young."

"That is not impossible," said Blade. "Certainly it is only quite recently that England has been sending out explorers such as myself to enter the other Cities of Peace. Mak'loh is the first one I have entered, and I had a long journey to reach it." Apparently she assumed that any civilized man in this Dimension had to be from another "City of Peace." Perhaps she was unable to conceive of any alternative. This was certainly a weakness, but it was a weakness very much to Blade's advantage for the moment.

"You came across the Warlands?" the woman said. She pointed at Blade's sword and knife as she spoke. Blade assumed she meant the lands outside the Wall.

"I did. That is why I brought those weapons you see. They are not as powerful as those of a City's Authority, but they do not attract so much attention from the Warlanders. And they are powerful enough, if one knows how to use them."

He put down the knife so that he was between it and the woman. Then he made his expression as severe as he could and spoke in a clipped, hard voice.

"You call this a City of Peace. Yet I crossed the Warlands

without shedding a drop of my blood. Only when I entered Mak'loh was I in real danger." In brisk sentences Blade told the tale of his adventures in this Dimension. He left out nothing, including Twana and the encounters with the Shoba's men. He merely implied that all of these things had happened *after* he'd reached Mak'loh with an exploring party.

As he talked, Blade noticed the woman's face turning pale and her breath coming more quickly. As he told of his encounter with the androids on the city wall, she shivered. When he told her of how he'd walked freely through this House of Peace and seen all that went on there, she put her hands over her face.

"I could have slain every man and woman in this building between sunset and dawn," Blade finished. "I did not, because I call them my brothers and sisters. Would the men of the Shoba be so kind, if they passed the Wall?"

The woman's voice came out muffled by her hands. "Blade—are you of the Authority, in England?"

"No. I am sent out by the Authority, as are the other explorers." To increase the pressure on the woman, he added, "I am no more than a common fighting man of England. It was a great honor for me to be chosen by the Authority, for there are many thousands of fighting men and women as skilled as I am."

"Th-th-thousands, like you?" the woman said, her voice starting to break. Blade nodded. "I'm surprised that you c-c-call us brothers and sisters. We—" and at that point her voice failed her completely. She turned over, buried her head in the pillows, and wept.

Blade said nothing but quietly moved closer to her and laid a hand on her shoulder. She didn't seem to notice it. Finally she wiped her eyes and rolled over, her hands clasped behind her head. Blade carefully kept his eyes off the slim white throat and the firm breasts thrusting up beneath the black coverall.

"I see Mak'loh has few secrets left from England," she said wearily. "The only way we could change the situation would be to kill you. You did not kill us, when you could have easily done so and perhaps thought we deserved it." There was a note of bleak despair in her voice. "So we will not kill you."

"Thank you," said Blade. He would have said it sarcastically, except for the genuine emotion in the woman's voice. Something about the situation of her city moved her deeply.

"Yet in England you seem to have forgotten where you came from," she went on. "So you will not understand Mak'loh until I tell you how the Cities of Peace came to be. Then perhaps we can understand each other better."

Blade smiled. "By all means, tell me." He'd be more than happy to sit and listen while the woman revealed all the secrets of Mak'loh, this city of the living dead.

Chapter 14

The woman's name was Sela, and she was one of the Council of the Authority of Mak'loh. The Authority consisted of several hundred selected and trained men and women. They were the only people in Mak'loh who led anything that might be called a normal life by Home Dimension standards. They were responsible for everything that might be needed to keep the city running and had to be done by human beings rather than by robots or androids.

They were a few hundred men and women. The total human population of Mak'loh was somewhere around a hundred thousand.

When Blade learned that, he felt he knew half the answer to why the city was slowly falling apart. He still needed to know how Mak'loh had ended up in this situation.

After listening to Sela for about five hours, Blade felt he knew.

A long time in the past—at least several thousand years ago—there had been a war in this Dimension. It had been an immensely destructive war, fought with nuclear weapons, bacteria, gas, and all the other resources of a highly technological civilization. A large part of that civilization had simply vanished in the war.

Part of it had somehow managed to survive, in spite of the destruction. There were comparatively few people left, but a large part of the Dimension's technological skills and resources still existed. This included the robots, the early models of android, and the very earliest models of the Inward Eye.

The Inward Eye was a method of directly stimulating the

101

human brain to give all the sensations of an actual experience while the individual slept. An enormous variety of incredibly vivid experiences could be recorded on tapes and reproduced with total fidelity, every sensation intact down to the last and smallest detail. All one needed to make one's sleeping hours more exciting than one's waking hours was an Inward Eye machine and a sufficiently large variety of tapes.

The black boxes with the wired helmets Blade had seen in the rooms above were Inward Eye machines. The early ones had been used both as a high-society hobby and a method of therapy in mental hospitals. Both high society and mental hospitals vanished during the war. The survivors were much too busy putting things back together to have any time for socializing or developing mental illnesses.

No matter how hard the human survivors worked, there still weren't enough of them. So the robots and androids became more and more essential. They became so essential that the manufacture and programming of robots and androids was one of the first industries to be revived. By the time civilization had recovered, the robots and androids outnumbered the people at least three to one.

It was then that a psychologist and scientist named Hudvom had a brilliant idea. At least it had seemed brilliant at the time, although Sela admitted she now very much doubted this. Blade was certain Hudvom's idea was the worst disaster to happen to this Dimension, except the Great War itself.

Hudvom counted the robots and androids. He observed that Inward Eye boxes and Inward Eye tapes were once again being made and used. He concluded that together they were the solution to the greatest problem facing his people.

That problem was preventing another war. War was the result of aggression. Aggression was the inevitable result of the amount and kind of physical activity that people performed. If they would limit themselves to the physical activity necessary to get work done, the problem wouldn't be so serious. But people were always in search of excitement, new sensations, pleasure, and variety. That search too often led them over the edge into a pattern of increasingly aggressive behavior.

102

Now there was at last a chance to break this deadly pattern. Much work was already being done by the robots and androids. More could be done. Meanwhile, people who wanted to could seek out a variety of sensations through new Inward Eye tapes. By this combination, the danger of people developing aggressive patterns of behavior would be greatly reduced. The danger of another war would be practically eliminated.

Hudvom was a brilliant and persuasive arguer, and people were already more than half ready to listen to him. There had already been small wars between some of the revived city-states. There were thousands of armed androids on hand. Many of the weapons that had made the Great War so terrible had already been rediscovered. Another major war seemed near, and this one would leave nothing alive in all the world.

So Hudvom was heard by thoroughly frightened people, and they thought him a great and wise man. The work began, to put Hudvom's ideas into effect.

The work was done slowly, over several centuries. Gradually the cities came to be inhabited by those who followed Hudvom's theories, who rejected the Physical, sought their sensations from the Inward Eye, and left everything else to the robots and the androids. Gradually those who thought Hudvom's theories were dangerous nonsense, or who simply couldn't adjust to the new way of life, left the cities. Some of them were forcibly expelled. All who left soon sank back to barbarism, as the cities kept a rigid control of all advanced science and technology.

In spite of their primitive weapons, the barbarians were numerous enough to be a danger to the cities. So the Cities of Peace slowly drew into themselves, building their walls and setting up force fields and robot sentinels to guard those walls. The building Blade had stayed in by the Wall had been built to house the human garrison of the Wall, in those distant centuries when such a garrison was needed. It had been abandoned by everyone except robots for more than a thousand years.

Gradually the cities became invulnerable to the attacks of the barbarians. Within five hundred years their life had settled down to a routine. Or at least the life of Mak'loh settled down to a routine. Sela knew practically nothing about what might have happened in the other Cities of Peace. Only three of them had ever sent visitors to Mak'loh, and none of these had come in Sela's lifetime. That lifetime, incidentally, had already lasted some four hundred years, and would probably last another five hundred.

In Mak'loh the routine became simple. The hundred thousand human beings in the city spent two-thirds of their time using the Inner Eye. There were millions of different tapes, and they could be mixed and varied by the computers. The other third of the time, they spent going languidly through various mild Physical activities that still helped to maintain a person's good health and good looks. Sometimes they even made love, although not often enough to produce very many children. At the moment there were in all of Mak'loh only seven nurseries and no more than three hundred children in all seven put together.

Meanwhile, computers, robots, and androids did everything else. The computers controlled the power supply, the protective force fields, the synthetic food factories. They programmed the robots and trained the androids.

The robots mounted guard on the outer Wall and took care of all the heavy maintenance. The androids in the red coveralls were soldiers, pure and simple, produced and trained to be nothing else. They lived in underground caves, connected with tunnels that ran under the whole city and up into the towers along the city wall.

The androids in blue did the thousand and one essential jobs in the city itself. Robots and androids together numbered over half a million, or about five for every human inhabitant of Mak'loh.

The Authority watched over everything. They had been created when the city built its Walls, as a force of trained people, capable of Physical activity, capable of aggression if necessary. They would be too few to use these qualities to endanger the city or themselves. But they would be enough to keep watch for minor accidents and failures and correct them. They would also be able to wake up the whole population of the city in an emergency, turning off the Inward Eyes, reprogramming the robots, retraining the androids, and so on.

At least that was the theory, and with the original thousand-man Authority, it might have worked in practice. Unfortunately, the appeal of the Inward Eye seduced away many members of the Authority. Old age took others. As the birth rate shrank, it became impossible to train enough new members of the Authority to replace those who'd gone. Century by century, the strength of the Authority shrank.

Eventually it shrank to the point where it could no longer do its job properly, and the slow decay of Mak'loh became more rapid. Errors crept into the programming of the robots and the training of the androids. This explained the mad soldier Blade had encountered on the city wall, the simple-minded responses of the Watchers, the deterioration of the gardens. Machines wore out and could no longer be replaced quickly, then could not be replaced at all. The power supply was sometimes erratic. Sometimes an Inward Eye machine would go wild, producing such intense sensations that a person hooked into it would be driven mad.

"At one time, about a century ago, it seemed that things were about to fall apart all at once," Sela said. "But all of us in the Authority made a tremendous effort and did much of the necessary work."

"It wasn't enough," said Blade.

The woman sighed. "This we know. We have known it for fifty years. But we were not strong enough to do any more. We are even weaker now. The only thing we could do to make any real difference would be to declare an emergency and turn off the Inward Eyes. We would have to cast aside all of Hudvom's teachings to do that. I fear the people would not accept that."

Blade suspected this was an excuse, rather than a reason, to justify the Authority's refusal to grasp the bull by the horns. The real problem was the pleasure the people of Mak'loh took in their carefree, sensual life of Inward Eye and android servants. They would continue to prefer their living death, even as their city fell apart around them. They would probably panic if they were awakened.

Blade didn't blame the Authority for not wanting to grab

105

this bull by the horns. It was a large and ferocious bull. But if they didn't quickly do something drastic, Mak'loh was doomed. It would become a city of the dead who no longer lived, even through the Inward Eye.

"This is true, I fear," said Sela. "But we of the Authority have given up hope. Even if we had hope, we lack the strength."

"Perhaps you lack the strength," said Blade. "But that does not mean that the strength does not exist or cannot be brought to Mak'loh."

"Will—will your comrades from England help us?" said Sela.

"Why not?" said Blade. "As I have said before, you are our brothers and sisters. From us you can learn how to bring Mak'loh back to life. From you we can learn our history and some of the science we have lost."

"That seems to be a fair bargain," said the woman, frowning. "But I cannot make promises for the whole Authority or speak for them all."

"I cannot do that for my comrades either," said Blade. "I shall have to see much more of your city before I can even speak to them. Show me Mak'loh, Sela. Take me everywhere in it, tell me everything you know about it, let me speak to the others of the Authority. Conceal nothing.

"When I have learned everything I can, I shall return across the Wall, to where my comrades wait in the Warlands. I shall speak to them and tell them what I have seen. I think they will agree to help your city. If they are not enough to do all that is needed, we will send word to England. That will bring more of our people to help Mak'loh."

Blade had never bluffed quite so extravagantly, and he wasn't entirely sure he'd be able to carry it off in the face of sharp wits like Sela's. Yet it was certainly his best chance of learning everything about Mak'loh, and perhaps in the end he could learn enough to actually give them some help.

Sela reached out and caught Blade's right hand in both of hers. There were tears in her eyes as she said, in a voice not entirely steady:

"Blade, we shall do what you wish. Mak'loh must live."

Chapter 15

Sela was as good as her word. She started by getting Blade the black coveralls of the Authority, as well as a combat helmet, boots, and gloves. She got him a new shock rifle and taught him how to use it more effectively. It could be set to either stun or kill, depending on how much power one wanted to use. She also warned Blade that some of the power cells could be unreliable, since the factory that made them was not working very well.

She also showed him the other main weapon kept in Mak'loh—one that was not given to the soldier androids. It was a grenade thrower that looked very much like a large-bore shotgun with a single, stubby barrel. Blade was familiar with similar weapons in Home Dimension, but this one was lighter and much more powerful. That explained why it was not given to the androids. Some time in the dim past, some wise man in the Authority had realized that the androids might not always be completely reliable and therefore should not have weapons as powerful as those of the Masters.

There were only about five hundred of the grenade throwers in Mak'loh, all of them firmly held by the Authority. Each thrower could fire a fist-sized grenade more than five hundred yards, and each grenade could blow a large tree to splinters or reduce a Watcher to scrap metal.

"There is not much ammunition for the throwers," said Sela apologetically. "The factory for the grenades has not been working for many years."

Blade sighed. "What were you planning to do if somebody *did* get in over the Wall and past the Watchers?" he asked irritably. "Spit at them?"

Sela had the grace to blush.

The last thing she gave Blade was not quite a weapon, although it did have warlike uses. It was a metal box to be slung on his belt, with controls and directional antennae that fastened onto his helmet. With a box he could neutralize the Watchers over a wide stretch of the Wall, or order them to concentrate and attack something they might otherwise ignore.

Blade was particularly careful to learn how to use the Watcher control. If necessary, the box would give him an easy passage over the Wall. Blade never minded having a line of retreat open, although he had no intention of retreating from Mak'loh.

After equipping Blade, Sela called up an escort of two soldiers and two workers. Then the two human beings and the four androids climbed into Sela's truck and rolled off on Blade's guided tour of Mak'loh.

They didn't bother with any of the Houses of Peace where most of the people lived. Blade had seen enough of those, and as he said, "When you've seen one House of Peace, you've seen them all."

What he wanted to see was the factories for weapons and machinery, food and clothing and furniture, robots, and trucks. He wanted to see where the androids were produced and trained for war and work. He wanted to see the sources for power, water, and the protective force fields. He wanted to learn how everything in Mak'loh worked or didn't work.

Sela showed him everything he asked to see, and the other men and women of the Authority were just as cooperative. The three people on duty at the force-field generators even showed him how to operate the master control panel.

"This controls the Dekim Field," a woman said, pointing at a quartet of dials set around a large switch. "The Dekim Field is radiated by coils set within the outer Wall, to give it strength to resist any explosions or sharp blows."

That explained why the Wall had stood firm against the exploding gunpowder, but not against the slow assaults of living plants. Blade couldn't help wondering what would happen if the Dekim Field were turned off.

There was also the Entesh Field, which produced the

golden shimmering above the Wall. It gave warning of intruders who reached the top and summoned the Watchers to deal with them. Once it had also been strong enough to keep out storms like the one that had covered Blade's and Twana's escape from the robots.

"That must have been quite a long time ago," said Blade drily.

"It was," Sela said.

Now the Entesh Field could only act as a sort of burglar alarm. Even then it depended heavily on the reliability of the Watchers—which was steadily deteriorating.

Finally, there was the Hoak Field, which produced the screen of blindness along the top of the Wall. That alone at times had been enough to keep Mak'loh safe from intruders from the Warlands outside.

"Anyone who was willing to feel his way along for another twenty-five feet could pass safely through the Hoak Field," said one of the men. "But the Warlanders had degenerated into superstitious barbarians, who would never be capable of such a thing."

Blade wondered if anybody in Mak'loh had ever seen the Shoba's men in action. No one he'd talked to had mentioned them, so he doubted it. The Shoba's trained soldiers might well be superstitious, but they were not barbarians, any more than the legions of Rome had been. Sooner or later, if the Shoba's army held together, it would be making a serious attempt on the Wall.

The main power plant of the city impressed Blade even more than the force-field generators. For one thing, the Authority people who ran the power plant and guarded it seemed to have escaped some of the apathy that had swallowed up their comrades. They were brisk, alert, and efficient. They also had several hundred picked android soldiers under their command. The Power Guard was the most highly trained fighting force Blade had seen in Mak'loh. "They must be the best," the woman in charge of their training said with a shrug. "How can they be otherwise? If the power dies, so does Mak'loh."

The power plant itself operated by the direct conversion of mass into energy. Theoretically, it could use any form of

109

mass, including sewage. In practice it was simpler to use heavy metals extruded into fine wire and fed into the converter.

Because of its abundance in this Dimension, gold was the favorite heavy metal. Blade saw the gold that was currently providing the power for the whole city—a bar that he could lift in one hand. He also saw the gold stored away for future needs—room after room of gold bars, stacked higher than a man. This mass of glittering metal would outweigh the combined gold reserves of every Home Dimension nation combined. At the present rate of consumption, Mak'loh had power for at least a thousand years. Ironic, when the city and everybody in it would be dead in less than half that time.

So it went, everywhere Blade traveled in Mak'loh. The city was a breathtaking and contradictory mixture of dazzling genius and creeping decay, with the decay slowly winning.

After a week of touring the city, Sela taught Blade how to use one of the Authority's flyers. The gravity-control fields in the Houses of Peace required heavy generators and a great deal of power. They could not be used in small flying machines. So the flyer was no more than a platform with controls slung between two ducted fans. It was easy to control, and the ones in service were all very carefully maintained. That was good news to Blade. As he put it:

"A thousand-foot fall can ruin a man's whole day."

Blade enjoyed the leisurely flights across the gardens, above the tops of Mak'loh's highest towers, even out to the Wall. There was no way to pass beyond the Wall, since the Hoak Field rose higher than the flyers could climb, and no man could control one of them blind. That did not worry Blade. He knew he had the measure of all Mak'loh's defenses, and none of them could prevent him from going where he wanted, when he wanted. This was vital to a plan that was rapidly taking shape in his mind.

It was a particularly lovely day, flawlessly clear from the moment the eastern sky began to turn pink with dawn. Blade and Sela were up early, bathing, breakfasting, and ordering the androids to prepare their flyer for the day's traveling.

They walked out to the landing platform as the sun crept

110

over the Wall. Overhead the sky was turning the pale blue that promised a scorching hot day. The android servant stowed away their lunch under the seat of the flyer, then climbed into the seat and strapped itself in.

Sela shook her head. "No, you will not be needed today."

"Yes, Master," said the android. "It unstrapped itself and vanished down the stairs. Sela turned to Blade and smiled.

"We are going farther than before today, into the western forests close to the Wall. It is so wild there that no one ever comes near it. Working androids do not know what to do there, so they are more of a nuisance than a help."

"I see," said Blade. By now he'd got used to the worker androids so they hardly seemed more than pieces of furniture. He was still happy to be free of them whenever possible.

Blade lifted the flyer off the platform, took it up above the highest tower of the city, and headed west. He flew slowly, his helmet off and his coveralls zipped open halfway down his chest. He savored the sunshine, the breeze, the gentle whirr of the fans, and the view below. From this high there was nothing to show that Mak'loh was a dying city, and all the colors of its towers blazed in the sunlight.

The city crept past below them; then came the inner wall and the gardens. They were green and luxuriant—too much so, with water plants choking streams, and ponds and creepers twining around trees. This was good land though— fertile and well-watered. With skilled cultivation, it could feed twice as many people as Mak'loh held now, and in time. . . .

No, he wouldn't let his mind spin fantasies of what could only lie in the distant future. There was little chance of Mak'loh turning back to the land for its food, and perhaps there would be no need to. Blade hoped so. The people of the city would have to do many things they were not doing now in order to survive, but they should not have to become sweating peasants. Not if his plan worked and the people of Mak'loh showed at least a little intelligence!

Half an hour later Blade sent the flyer spiraling down to a landing on the edge of the forest along the western Wall. He couldn't land in the forest itself without the risk of impaling the flyer on a treetop.

The flyer touched down, and the fans whispered into

silence. Blade and Sela climbed down to the ground, hoisted their gear, and strode into the forest.

They walked a mile through the hot, windless silence under the trees, brushing off insects and rapidly working up a sweat. At last they broke out of the trees onto the bank of a small stream. It flowed down a hillside between two grassy banks, clear and cold, so fast that the water plants hadn't been able to choke it. Flowering bushes like lilacs dotted the hillside, rising twelve and fifteen feet, covering the grass with fallen yellow blossoms and filling the air with a delicate sweet scent. It was an absolutely irresistible place for a picnic.

Blade dropped the gear, while Sela sat down and pulled off her boots. She lay back on the grass, wiggling her toes, hair spread out around her head, the picture of absolute contentment. Suddenly she sat up and began undoing her coveralls. "Blade, I think I'll take a bath in the stream before we eat. I feel like I've been cooked along with the mush in one of the food factory's raw material vats."

"Can you swim?" Blade had to ask. He'd never seen Sela enter the water, or indeed do anything without at least her coverall and boots on. He'd always been aware of the body under those coveralls, but he'd never seen it.

Before he could complete the thought, Sela's coveralls were lying on the grass beside her boots. She stood up, wearing a sort of padded green body stocking. Her figure hardly needed padding. Blade assumed it was some sort of protective garment, like the bulletproof vests worn by the android soldiers. She reached around behind her and tried to undo the neck of the vest. Her fingers waved desperately an inch short of the seal.

She laughed in amused frustration. "This is the first time in years I've tried to take off one of these things without an android to help me. Could you help me, Blade?"

Blade stepped over behind Sela and gently undid the neck of the vest. Even more gently he undid the seam down her back, until he could see an expanse of creamy skin stretching all the way down to the cleft between her buttocks. A second glance told him that skin was lightly freckled. He let his hands rest on the back of her neck for a moment. Then he pushed the vest slowly down off her shoulders. She stood without moving or even breathing hard as it slipped down to her waist. Then she turned around.

Against the freckled whiteness of her breasts, her large nipples were startlingly dark. Blade raised his hands, ran them down her neck and over her shoulders to her breasts, brushed his thumbs lightly across the nipples, felt them harden and rise. Sela still did not move, but her breasts seemed to take on a life of their own as her breathing quickened.

It had been almost inevitable that sooner or later they would come together like this. Blade had been too aware of Sela's beauty not to be showing interest. Sela was experienced enough to notice those signs of interest. To be sure, she hadn't had an actual Physical sex experience in more than fifty years. Those of the Authority had many more waking hours free of the Inward Eye, but they also had much more work to do. Besides, they seldom found anyone but another member of the Authority a congenial bed partner.

Sela continued to stand motionless while Blade worked on her with both his lips and his hands. His lips crept up and down her body from throat to navel, lingering the longest on her breasts, drawing her nipples out, making the skin around them flush. His hands slowly shoved the vest down past her waist, her hips, her thighs, until it slid on its own down her legs to fall in a pile at her feet. She still stood motionless as Blade stepped back from her long enough to strip off his own coverall. He wore nothing under it but a padded loinguard, and then nothing at all.

This time Sela moved when she felt his hands on her. Her kiss began as tentatively and fumbling as the first kiss of a schoolgirl, but did not stay like that for long. There was little skill in it, but there was a passion ready to be given with no thought of holding back. Blade's mouth opened to meet Sela's, and his arms went around her as hers gripped him.

They stood like that for a time that neither could measure, lips on lips, hands everywhere and anywhere on each other's bodies. Blade's hands gripped Sela's firm buttocks, while her hands strayed from the small of his back into his groin. Blade felt a rising heat there and felt dampness in the fine hair between Sela's thighs. That hair seemed to have a life of its

113

own as it curled around Blade's rising erection, enticing, inflaming, maddening.

The madness was more than either could continue to endure where they were. Blade wasn't sure whether they lay down of their own free will or whether their knees simply folded under them. He found himself on his back in the grass, while Sela straddled his thighs and slid down upon him in the same moment that he thrust smoothly up into her. There was a moment's tension, a moment's resistance, then an easy joining. For another moment Blade held himself absolutely still, terribly certain that with Sela's warmth around him he would explode if he made a single movement. Then the matter was out of his control, as Sela began to move upon him.

She moved up and down and from side to side, twisting all of her body from her thighs up to her head. She threw her head forward until her hair flowed down over her breasts, then threw it back until the hair flowed down to the base of her spine. She tossed her arms about, clutching now at Blade, now at the empty air, now burying her fingers in her hair, now stroking her own breasts. She seemed to be turning from a woman into an animal, and then into something that was not even flesh and blood, only passion cleverly disguised.

As she changed, Sela drew Blade steadily after her, until he could not be sure that he was still part of the world around him. All his being was becoming part of the woman above him, as all of her being was becoming part of him.

They merged until it seemed that their bodies must blur, melt, and run together. In that moment they reached their peak, held that peak for another moment, then fell down the other side of it with flame before their eyes and thunder roaring in their ears. They could not have told one moment from another and one sensation from another to save their lives.

Slowly the world around them returned. Blade felt grass prickling against his bare skin, sweat trickling down it, the breeze on his face, the warmth and softness and weight of Sela sprawled across him. He raised his head enough to see that she was sound asleep, little gasps from her open mouth stirring the hair on his chest. It seemed to Blade that Sela was doing a sensible thing, and he did the same.

Eventually they woke and took the baths that had been so pleasantly delayed. They were hungry after that and emptied the picnic box in record time. Their hands met as they stowed away the plates and bottles, and the meeting of the hands awoke desire again.

They spent all afternoon making love there by the stream. Blade saw how the sunlight creeping through the leaves dappled Sela's body, how her lips danced with exquisite abandon up and down his body, how bits of leaves got caught in her hair as it grew steadily more tangled.

Eventually the afternoon came to an end. Blade had reached his limits, and Sela was getting ravenously hungry. Since the nearest food was more than forty miles away in Mak'loh, there was nothing to do but pack up and go home.

They flew back to the city as the western sky began to glow red. Blade flew in a complete circle around the city before landing. He contemplated the new and marvelous colors the sunset gave to the soaring towers. He also contemplated the best way of using a flyer in his plan to release Mak'loh from its living death.

Sela laid a hand on his arm and smiled. It was a lazy, sensuous, satisfied smile, warm with memory and also with anticipation. It told Blade a great deal. Above all, it told Blade that Sela had no intention of letting another fifty years go by before she joined Physically with a man. In fact, she wasn't going to wait even fifty hours.

He'd brought her to a new awareness of the delights of the Physical, and now she was half in love with him, or at least half addicted to him. So she might take what he was about to do to her city as the grossest treachery, a blow too brutal to endure.

Blade didn't like the thought, but he didn't see that he had any real choice. Mak'loh was too far gone for there to be any safe or easy way to save it.

Chapter 16

Blade waited until Sela was so deeply asleep in the great bed that an earthquake couldn't have awakened her. Then he slipped out of the bed, went out into the corridor, and ran to the room where he'd left his equipment.

He quickly pulled it on. There was a complete combat outfit, from helmet to boots, including a shock rifle, grenade thrower, sack of extra grenades and power cells, and a Watcher control. It was just possible that by morning every man and woman in the city of Mak'loh would be ready to kill him on sight and there would be nothing he could do to change their minds. In that case, staying around would be a singularly pointless form of suicide and a quick retreat over the Wall into the Warlands the only sensible thing to do.

Neither androids nor human beings paid any attention to Blade as he walked down the corridor and rode up the shaft to the roof of the building. Some of the people in the Houses of Peace were vaguely aware that there was a stranger in Mak'loh, a man said to be from another of the Cities of Peace where life was very different from what it was here. More Physical, or so the rumors ran. However, no one had been sufficiently curious about this Physical stranger to speak to him.

That would certainly change tonight. By dawn everyone in Mak'loh would have heard of Richard Blade of England, no matter what they thought of him.

He stepped out on the roof, walked to his flyer, and checked it carefully. He'd loaded it with extra food and water, extra power cells for the fan motors, a tent sewn together out of old robes and blankets, and a sleeping bag. He

117

might be able to fly out of Mak'loh tonight, if he did have to leave. In that case, why not fly out ready to live as comfortably as possible until he returned to Home Dimension? Blade was not a man to run around naked and live on raw meat merely for his own amusement.

He lifted the flyer into the night sky and climbed until it would be impossible to see him and hard to hear him from the ground. Then he set a course for the field-generator building and flew slowly and levelly.

He would have to succeed the first time, or not at all. Even if he personally survived a failure tonight, he would have lost the necessary advantage of surprise. All the vital installations would be heavily defended and the Authority on the alert. The soldier androids might not be very good, but there were far too many of them for one man to face if they had orders to deal with him.

Over the industrial area of the city, Blade dropped to roof-top height and slowed down until he was practically drifting along. At last he saw the six-hundred-foot tower that held the generators for the force fields looming out of the darkness ahead. He climbed slightly, skimmed in over the edge of the roof, and landed. Instantly he was out of the flyer and flattening himself on the rough pebbled surface of the roof. He lay searching the darkness until he was certain that the roof was empty.

Blade had landed on the roof because he expected it to be unguarded, not because it was closest to the control room. That lay five hundred feet down a spiraling ramp. From the control room, another ramp led to the ground level. A dozen androids guarded that ramp. It was assumed that no one could possibly come down from above except other members of the Authority, and they could not possibly be dangerous to anything or anyone in Mak'loh.

Blade fixed his bayonet, raised his rifle, and began to descend the ramp. The rifle was set to stun, and he carried two fused gas grenades in his belt. Over his nose and mouth he wore one of the Authority's gas masks, a transparent sheet of plastic-like filtering material no heavier than a pocket handkerchief. Yet it would protect him completely from a gas that could kill an unprotected human being in thirty seconds.

118

The ramp was well-lit, and Blade could have gone much faster than he did. Instead, he waited at each turn, listening for the slightest noise from ahead. He heard only the distant pulsing of the field generators that came steadily through the solid walls. He saw only the ramp and walls, bare except for small doors that led into the generator compartments. He was able to measure his downward progress by reading off the markings on the doors.

A hundred feet down from the roof. Two hundred. Three hundred. It began to seem impossible that there could be any-one waiting for him, when all the lights went out. He hit the floor before the after-images faded from his eyes. As he stretched out, he heard feet climbing out of the darkness toward him. Blade unhooked one of the gas grenades from his belt and, without pulling the pin, sent it rolling down the ramp toward the oncoming footsteps.

It clattered away into the darkness. The footsteps halted. Then the white flare of rifle fire lit up the ramp. He'd drawn the fire to the approaching people, as he'd hoped to.

Aiming by sound in the darkness, the unknown rifleman made a good shot—good enough to burst the grenade. It went off with a sharp crack, followed by the *spannnng* of fly-ing fragments and the *wsssssh* of escaping gas. A woman screamed.

Blade leaped to his feet and followed up the grenade. He rounded the bend as the lights came back on again. The ramp ahead was hazy with the yellow-green gas. Beyond the cloud of gas were two people in Authority coveralls. On the right a woman sat leaning against the wall, clawing at her throat. Her head was thrown back, and her eyes rolled franti-cally upward. A fragment of the grenade had torn open her cheek and her gas mask, letting a lethal dose of the gas into her lungs.

On the left lay a man, staring as Blade came around the bend. With skill and precision, he snapped up his rifle and fired. Blade was already diving for the floor, squeezing the trigger of his own rifle, as the beam cracked past his head. Blade's own shot took the man in the leg.

Before the man could fire again, Blade rolled over and came up on his knees. They were too close now to fire. The man brought his rifle up to guard against a blow at his chest or throat. Blade went in over the man's guard with his bayonet, thrusting at his face and ripping open his mask. The man screamed. Blade reversed his rifle and cracked the man across the jaw with the butt, stunning him. He slumped back against the wall, dying more quietly than the woman as the gas ate into his lungs.

Blade sprang to his feet and plunged down the ramp at a dead run. It didn't matter whether or not there were anyone else waiting in ambush. He couldn't afford to waste a second. The noise of the fight must have alerted the people in the control room. He might have to kill them, and that would absolutely be the end of his chances for staying in Mak'loh after tonight. Damn it, he hadn't wanted anybody killed at all! There wouldn't have been, either, if these two clowns hadn't ambushed him—and where the devil had they come from anyway?

By the time Blade finished asking himself these questions, he was almost down to the level of the control room. He covered the last few yards of the ramp flattened against the wall. The control team was seated at the board, each man with a rifle across his knees. Only one had his eyes on the board. The other two were looking at the entrances to the upward and downward ramps. Blade raised his rifle and aimed it at the three. The movement caught one man's eye. He shouted and started to jump up.

At that moment, running feet sounded on the ramp from the ground floor. Two more armed men in Authority coveralls burst into view, and behind them six soldier androids. One of them saw Blade and shouted to the androids:

"Kill the Warlander!"

The time it took the man to shout was enough for Blade to act. He stunned the man who'd shouted, then dropped flat as the androids sent white fire crackling over his head. The walls and ceiling smoked and cracked where the beams struck. Those rifles were set to kill. Apparently those androids had been told Blade was no Master but a Warlander. That made him fair game.

Seeing androids firing on someone *he* knew to be a Master, one of the men at the control board sprang out of his chair, firing at the androids. He knocked out two of them and spoiled the aim of the other four. The second human attacker promptly shot the control man. The blast reduced his head to a charred ruin.

In the confusion, Blade dashed across the control room. The androids saw him but didn't fire. They couldn't risk hitting the control board or one of the Masters at it. Blade went over the top of the control board like a high jumper and dropped to his knees on the floor behind it. The two surviving control men threw themselves out of their seats, not sure what was going on but sure they didn't want to get killed in it. The surviving attacker had to climb over one of them to get around the control board at Blade. By the time he'd done this, Blade had his rifle aimed and fired with the muzzle almost against the man's chest. The man flew a foot into the air, then crashed to the floor.

The four surviving androids milled around without firing. They faced a situation not covered in their training, with no orders coming from their Masters or any others. Blade stunned one of them, and that persuaded the other three to turn and run off down the ramp toward the ground level. Blade took a high-explosive grenade, set the fuse for a delayed detonation, and fired it down the ramp after the fleeing androids. Silence followed the explosion.

Cautiously the two surviving control men rose to their feet. They looked at their dead comrade, the fallen humans and androids, and Blade standing by the board.

"What in the name of Peace is going on?" said one of them furiously. He started to sit down in his seat.

"There are going to be some changes made in this city tonight," said Blade politely and tapped the man on the head with the butt of his rifle. Before the other control man could react, Blade fired and stretched him out on the floor along with everybody else.

On one side of the room was a large freight elevator that ran from top to bottom of the building. Blade opened the door and shoved all the bodies from both sides, human and android alike, into the elevator. Then he sent the elevator down to the ground level and locked the controls. That should keep everyone safe and out of his hair for the next few minutes. He could sort out who had been trying to do what to whom afterward.

The control room opened on one side onto a balcony that ran around a vast circular chamber, more than two hundred feet across and a hundred feet high. In the center of the chamber, a gleaming steel column fifty feet in diameter rose to vanish in the ceiling. Inside that column lay the working parts of various field generators, stacked one on another in a pile more than five hundred feet high. Around the base of the column was a glittering array of consoles, conduits, displays, switchboards, and piping. There were the essential monitors and power relays for the generators.

If they were destroyed, it would take five years to rebuild them. Until they were rebuilt, the field generators could no longer be powered or controlled safely. The three force fields would no longer protect Mak'loh. Its people would have to look to their own protection, however much this cost them in Physical activity. In five years it was possible that the city would be firmly set on a new course, freer of android servants and the pleasures of the Inward Eye.

It was no more than just possible, but it was the best chance Blade could give this city.

He went to the control board and carefully closed the master switched for all three fields. Every light on the board flashed from green to red, then died entirely. Wrecking the controls with the fields still active could do even more permanent damage, but it might also set off an explosion like an atomic bomb. Blade did not want to wake up Mak'loh by laying half of it in ruins.

Blade walked out on to the balcony, the loaded grenade thrower in his hands. He stood by the railing, sighted on the nearest console, and fired. He dropped to the floor as the grenade exploded, ripping the console to bits and spraying pieces of metal and circuitry in all directions.

Blade worked his way around the balcony as methodically as a farmer planting seed. Explosion after explosion ripped through the equipment below. The lights went out, and emergency lighting came on with dim glows like fireflies. A few more explosions, and the emergency lights also went out.

Blade pulled a flashlight out of his pack and went on shooting by its light.

Explosions blazed orange and circuits flared up blue-white in the darkness. Metal fragments rained down around Blade, skittered off the balcony, clanged and cracked into the walls. Smoke swirled around Blade like fog, carrying a stench of high explosive, burned insulation, and melted metal.

Blade ran out of targets long before he ran out of grenades. Then he climbed down a ladder from the balcony to the floor of the chamber. He'd done a very adequate job with the time and the equipment he'd had.

There was only one more thing to do. Blade flashed his light at the main control board high above. Then he aimed the thrower and fired. The first grenade blew the board off its mountings. The second blew it in half and threw two of the chairs off the balcony. Blade was reloading again when a voice called out of the darkness. He stopped, the grenade in one hand.

He wasn't surprised to hear voices. What the voice was saying did surprise him.

Sharp and demanding, the voice in the darkness called out, "Blade, stop firing! We're on your side!"

Chapter 17

Blade's first thought was that either his hearing or his brain had been damaged by the grenade explosions. By sheer reflex he dropped the third grenade into the thrower. In the silence after the explosion, the *click* echoed all around the chamber.

The man above heard it. "Get back, you fools!" he shouted. "He may fire again!" Blade heard the sound of several sets of retreating feet. "Damn you, Blade," came the voice again. "I told you we're friends. We're from the Authority."

Blade took cover behind a metal cabinet standing on end. "That's not enough," he shouted back. "I've already had to defend myself tonight against four people in Authority clothing. How do I know that I can trust you?"

"We know about the fight," the man said. "We've got the people you put in the elevator. I swear it; you've nothing to fear from us."

By now Blade recognized the voice. It was Geetro, a member of the Authority Council and the man in charge at the main power station. He was one of the more alert minds, even among the power-plant tenders.

Yet that didn't mean he could be trusted. Something was going on in Mak'loh that seemed to have produced open warfare among factions of the Authority. Which faction was Geetro's?

"Turn on a light," Blade shouted. "Then leave it on and come down here. We'll talk privately."

"You want us to give you a target?" shouted another voice from behind Geetro. "You're a damned fool if—"

"Oh, be quiet, the whole lot of you," said a woman's voice. The voice was Sela's.

"Sela!" Blade shouted.

"Blade! It *is* all right. I swear it. Geetro is the leader of—"

"Enough, Sela! We'll talk of that in private, if you don't mind. Blade, will you come up now?"

Blade still had no idea what Geetro might be planning, but if Sela were willing to trust him that would have to be enough. Blade stepped out from behind the cabinet, walked to the ladder, and climbed up to the balcony.

As he reached the top, somebody turned on a powerful light, revealing the whole chamber. He saw a cluster of armed men and women in Authority black standing in the control room. As they saw the shambles Blade had left behind him, some shouted furiously, while others turned toward Blade with dark looks on their faces.

Geetro and Sela restored order and came toward Blade. Geetro held out a hand, and Blade noticed that the hand was sweaty and trembled slightly. The man was not quite as much in charge of the situation as he pretended to be. They shook hands, and Geetro looked down at the wrecked control equipment with a sour smile. "Well, Blade, I could wish we'd been able to get by without you doing this, but—"

"Geetro, you know how little hope there was of that," said Sela briskly. "So stop trying to prove how mild you are. We've gone too far for that to make any difference, and it certainly won't impress Blade. Not after he's done this." Her hand made a sweeping gesture that took in the whole chamber.

"I suppose you are right," said Geetro. "Will you come with us, Blade? We will not force you. But I think you will want to find out what is going on, and I know you will be safer with us and our androids guarding you."

"Very well," said Blade. "I came here in a flyer though. It's up on the roof, with my—"

"Blade," said Geetro, an edge in his voice. "Forget your flyer. This building will be guarded from the ground and from the roof as soon as the androids of the Power Guard arrive. Besides, it is no longer a target that Paron—that the other people will be attacking. You've done your work so well that it's no longer *worth* anything." A couple of the men growled in irritable agreement, then fell silent at a glare from Sela. "Blade, *come*."

Blade fell in behind Geetro and headed down the ramp.

They led Blade to a truck and followed a zigzag course through back streets and alleys to the power plant. The plant was guarded by androids standing almost shoulder to shoulder. Some of them wore the badge of the Power Guard on their coveralls, and these seemed to be giving orders to the others. All the androids had the usual shock rifles and truncheons, and some of the Power Guard were carrying grenade throwers.

"That is against the old laws," said Geetro. "But we are now in a time of new laws for Mak'loh. It is a time we hoped might come sooner or later. You have brought it many years sooner than we expected." He said nothing more to explain those cryptic words until they were all safely inside the main control room of the power plant. Then they sat down, took off their weapons and gear, and ate a light meal. While they ate, Geetro and Sela talked. By the time they'd finished the meal, Blade had a fairly good idea of what was happening in Mak'loh.

Not everyone in the Authority accepted the decline of the city as passively as Blade had believed. Twenty years before, Geetro conceived almost the same idea as Blade. Attack something vital in Mak'loh, something so vital that its destruction would bring about a crisis in the city. Then the people would have to choose between death and setting aside the life of the Inward Eye.

"It took me nearly all those twenty years to find thirty people I could trust," said Geetro. "I did not want to try anything with a smaller number."

Blade tactfully refrained from asking why Geetro hadn't realized that one man in the right place at the right time could do the job. In any case, he knew the answer. A man of Mak'loh had enough trouble conceiving the idea in the first place. There was no point in blaming Geetro for not doing something he would have found almost completely impossible, for psychological reasons.

127

"Eventually I had my thirty. I also knew there were about fifty more among the Authority who would be on my side once I had taken the first vital step. Sela was among them."

"I see," said Blade. He gave Sela a hard look. "Did you know anything of what Geetro had in mind when you were showing me around?" He did not care for the possibility that she'd been systematically deceiving him.

"I did not *know*," she said calmly. "I suspected that he had a plan. I suspected that, if he did have a plan, it would be something like this. He was not the only one with the wits to understand what Mak'loh needed. I will admit he was the only one with the courage necessary—until you came. Yet I did not show you around the city with the idea of helping you to do what you have done tonight. I believed what you said, about bringing in your comrades to help us. I thought that would be a much better way, and we would not have to destroy anything." Her shoulders sagged. "Blade, did *you* lie to me—about being one of many explorers from England?"

"I did not lie about that," said Blade. He realized he was going to have to make a few changes in his story now that Sela was politely calling his bluff. "I was. Three parties set out from England, with six men in each one. We traveled separately, and my party was the first to reach Mak'loh. I do not know where the other two parties are. They may be dead."

"How is this?" said Geetro, surprised. "It has been a long time since anyone in the Warlands could harm people from the Cities of Peace."

"Times have changed," said Blade. "The Warlands beyond Mak'loh's Wall are ruled by a man called the Shoba. I do not know what kind of man he is, but I know what kind of army he has." He repeated to Geetro what he'd told Sela about the Shoba's army.

"They were good enough to kill two of my comrades and wound two more so that they could not travel. I left one man with the wounded and came on myself, into the Warlands villages where I met the girl Twana. Then we came on, over the Wall and into Mak'loh. I have no way of calling my comrades. I do not even know that the Shoba's men have not found them and killed them. Here in Mak'loh I was alone,

128

and I knew I would be alone for a long time. I knew that I could do what was necessary alone, and that the sooner I did it the better. The rest you have seen tonight."

"We have," said Geetro, "and I suppose we must be grateful to you for it."

"You certainly ought to be," said Sela. "The job is done, without you having to gather your own courage to do it or dirty your own hands by doing it yourself."

"You've spoken truly," said Geetro. "The job is done, and by a man who—" He broke off suddenly, but not before his voice had taken on a tone that Blade recognized and distrusted. Quietly Blade dropped one hand to the butt of his rifle and shifted in his chair so that he could leap to his feet in a hurry.

Sela also recognized Geetro's tone and finished the sentence. "And by a man who is not of us, and can therefore be blamed—and punished—for it without danger. That is what you think. That is what I see on your face and hear in your voice.

"Think again, Geetro. You will not prove how clean your own hands are by washing them in the blood of this man. Not when he had the courage to do alone what you did not have the courage to do with thirty people behind you."

Geetro sucked in his breath. "Is there—love—between you and Blade, Sela?" Blade hadn't expected to find plain, simple jealousy in Mak'loh, but it was all over Geetro's face. He sincerely hoped Sela would answer, "No," and be telling the truth when she did.

"No," said Sela, with a thin smile. "You do not need to worry about that, Geetro. But you do need to worry about what may happen if you try to kill Blade. He has proved that he can deal very well with any attack coming at him from the front. As for taking him from the rear—any blow at his back must pass through me to reach him." She laid her rifle across her knees.

Blade had the strong feeling that the meeting was about to degenerate, if not into violence, at least into pointless squabbling. He raised his voice. "This is not telling me much of what I need to know, Geetro. Or have you decided to kill me

129

so that I will not need to know anything more? If so, Sela is right. I will not be easy to kill."

Geetro clutched his hair with both hands, as though he wanted to pull it out by the roots in large handsful. "No, no, no! Blade, Sela, enough! We are not going to kill you."

"Very good," said Blade. "So let us talk of other things. Who is Paron?"

Paron was, or at least had been, the chief of the Authority people responsible for the production, programming, and training of the robots and androids. He was also one of the very few really original and creative thinkers left in Mak'loh, although his originality and creativity had led him into strange and dangerous paths.

Paron's new programs for the worker androids had greatly increased their skills. He had even done some experiments with the training of the soldier androids, to make them more able to act without orders. Those new training methods could also make the soldiers much more dangerous to the human inhabitants of Mak'loh, or so the Authority had come to believe. They outlawed Paron's experiments and confiscated all his experimental androids. They hadn't dared to do more than that. Paron was too indispensable to the working of the robot and android factories. That was unfortunate. They had merely shamed and angered Paron, enough to give him a strong desire for revenge without depriving him of the ability to take that revenge when he chose.

Still, Paron was a man of Mak'loh. Like Geetro, he came very slowly to the idea of doing anything that would upset or force a change in the city's way of life. He acquired a faction of supporters, but neither he nor they had any clear idea of what they ought to do. He was vaguely aware that Geetro was forming a faction of his own, for some purpose or purposes, but couldn't begin to guess what those purposes might be.

At this point Blade began to wonder if either side in this fight were competent to run a dockside tavern, let alone a city or a revolution.

Enter Richard Blade. Paron realized at once that Blade was something new and unpredictable. At the very least he might be dangerous as a rallying point for Geetro's faction.

In any case he had to be guarded against. So Paron started putting some of his people secretly on watch around some of the key buildings in Mak'loh. (It was those people Blade had fought in the field-generator building.)

Geetro's people noticed what Paron was doing and became suspicious. Geetro himself began to wonder if Paron was not hatching some sort of counterplot. So he started having some of his own people on alert each night, ready to move into action on short notice. In another year he might even have worked up the courage to forestall Paron and take over all the important buildings himself.

Blade prayed mentally for patience. These people had an awesomely advanced science and technology. When it came to politics, they were like frightened children cowering in the corner of a darkened room, afraid the bogeyman would get them.

Before anybody could get up the courage to do anything more, Richard Blade walked into the control room for the field generators and blew everything to bits. He smashed not only irreplaceable hardware but many years of planning by both factions. In plain language, he'd started a full-scale civil war in Mak'loh.

It was going to be a remarkably peculiar civil war, thought Blade. There might be no more than two or three hundred people fighting out of more than a hundred thousand in the city. Some of the people from the Houses of Peace might join in, but not many and not soon. Even when they did, how many of them would be of any use?

However, the situation could have been a great deal worse. He himself was still alive and no longer alone. Even the support of fifty or so well-intentioned amateur revolutionaries was better than nothing. If they would take his advice, he might be able to help them become a fairly potent force.

Except for the robot and android factories, all the important installations in Mak'loh were now held by Geetro's people or by androids who would take orders from no one but Geetro. The androids would stun any other Masters and kill their soldiers outright.

In fact, Geetro had a considerable edge in android fighting strength. By a strange irony, most of Paron's experimental androids had been assigned to the Power Guard after being confiscated. So Geetro had most of Paron's own android brain children as part of his fighting force. These androids were capable of using grenade throwers—at least on other androids. They could also act as sergeants and even officers to other androids.

Paron, on the other hand, had nothing except conventional androids on his side. "That's not entirely accidental," said Geetro. "We were watching him rather closely for any signs of more experiments in android training. If he'd done anything unusual, we might have moved against him at once."

"That would have been wise," said Blade. "Also, what happens now, when Paron still controls the robot and android factories? You can no longer keep watch on him. What happens if he starts producing androids capable of killing Masters?"

That remark produced a dead silence. Geetro swallowed. "He would not take the risk. The people of Mak'loh would turn against him in a moment if he did."

"The people of Mak'loh aren't going to be turning anywhere except over in bed for several weeks," said Blade sharply. "Plenty of time for a desperate man to do a great deal of damage."

"He could not possibly become that—"

"He certainly could become that desperate," said Blade. "He has only two choices now—win or die." He paused, then added in a level voice, "So do we."

The others looked blankly at him for a moment, then slowly nodded. Geetro was the first to speak.

"Very well, Blade. You of England seem to know more of this sort of thing than we of Mak'loh. You promised us your help to save our city. Tell us what to do, and we shall listen."

Chapter 18

Blade expected that open war would explode throughout Mak'loh within a few days. Blundering and inept warfare, perhaps, with both sides learning as they went along, but savage. Armies did not have to be skilled in order to be bloodthirsty.

In fact, almost nothing happened for several weeks. Each side started by establishing a sort of fortified camp, too strong to be attacked by the other without heavy losses. Each side took care to block off the underground tunnels leading into their camp, so that any attacks would have to be delivered on the surface.

Paron made his camp in the robot and android factory. Geetro made his camp in the power plant. Each side tried to win over as many as possible of the uncommitted Authority people. Each side sent out patrols through the city, on foot and in trucks, and occasionally sent flyers over the other's camp. Each side sniped at the other's androids, sometimes hitting them, and collected as many weapons as they could.

Neither side seriously tried to inflict casualties on the other's humans. Neither side tried to interfere with the movements and work of the uncommitted Authority people. The Walls were as well patrolled and the Houses of Peace as well served as ever.

It was a classical stand-off. Blade realized that neither side could think of a way to gain an advantage that didn't risk leaving the city defenseless or destroying something vital. Only part of this was a reasonable concern for their fellow citizens in the Houses of Peace. Much of it was a continued fear of rocking the boat too badly—even it it were sinking under their feet.

Left to himself, Blade would have organized a full-scale attack on the robot and android factory. He was reasonably certain that the Power Guard androids would give Geetro's side a decisive advantage. Of course, there would still have to be a pitched battle, and the factory might even be destroyed in the fighting. Blade certainly hoped so. He didn't want to destroy the androids and robots already in existence. They were too badly needed for too many essential jobs and would be needed for many years to come. But if no more were manufactured for a generation or two, Blade couldn't see any harm in that.

Geetro, however, wouldn't accept such a bold plan. Sela might have done so, but she was being very careful to avoid the appearance of allying herself with Blade against Geetro. The man's jealousy could too easily warp his judgment and put Blade in danger.

It was amusing to realize that Geetro might be the first man in Mak'loh to "fall in love" in the past century or so. It wasn't so amusing that it added one more complication to Blade's job, when he had enough already.

In spite of Geetro's refusal to plan a major offensive, Blade did not let time go to waste. All the sudden uproar and confusion in the city drew the notice of several thousand people from the Houses of Peace. Many of them wandered out into the streets of Mak'loh for the first time in a couple of centuries, willing to exert themselves Physically to satisfy their curiosity. Most of these wanderers met Geetro's people first.

Blade and Sela were able to recruit several hundred of them for Geetro's little army. They didn't try talking about a duty to the future of Mak'loh. The more intelligent ones would figure that out for themselves, and trying to convince the others would be a waste of breath and a waste of time. Instead, Blade and Sela pointed out that staying awake and moving about freely for a whole month could offer a whole new set of sensations, different from any available on an Inward Eye tape.

"And if there is fighting against Paron's androids," Blade added, "you will be in *combat*. Combat gives incredibly vivid sensations, like nothing else in the world." That was the truth, if not exactly the whole truth.

The new recruits were enthusiastic, but they had to be trained completely from scratch. "They hardly know which end of the rifle to hold and which to aim," was the way Blade put it. He found himself having to spend several hours a day training the new recruits until they were at least as dangerous to the enemy as to their own comrades.

Fortunately, the rest of Geetro's developing army did not require Blade's help. With only a few orders and a minimum of supervision, the Power Guard androids could train other androids well enough. Geetro's personal followers spent so much time on patrol duty that they learned the business of soldiering almost in spite of themselves. Blade actually had time to spare, and he put that time into improving the weapons of Geetro's army.

The rifles and grenade throwers were good enough for the jobs they were designed to do. Paron's androids had carried away much of the reserve stocks of weapons and ammunition, so for the moment they were somewhat better armed than Geetro's people. But Geetro had the weapons factory, and the assembly lines were being reprogrammed and started up again. Geetro would soon have an advantage in "conventional" weaponry.

What Blade wanted to create was something unconventional—at least in terms of this war and this Dimension. So he reinvented the mortar.

As he explained it to Geetro:

"It's just a metal tube, closed at one end. You put a can of explosives—called a shell—into the tube. Then you fire it. The shell rises high into the air, so the mortar can even be hidden behind a building. When the shell lands, it explodes like a grenade, only it's much bigger and more destructive."

"How can you know where the shell lands, if you fire from behind a building?" asked Sela. "Does someone stand up on top of the building and tell the mortar people?"

Blade grinned. "You've got it exactly right. Each mortar needs not only a crew, but what we call in England a 'forward observer.' We will have to train these, as well as build the mortars. So it's time we got started."

The industrial computers could turn any set of specifications into workable designs and then program the machine tools in the factories to build it. The problem was the shortage of competent computer programmers, reliable computers, and well-maintained machinery. Blade knew he would not be exactly popular in Mak'loh if the first mortar blew up and took its crew with it, so he insisted on taking everything slowly and carefully.

It was two weeks before the first mortar and shell were ready for testing. The mortar was a heavy, monstrously ugly thing that looked as if it had been made in a boiler factory and needed four strong men to carry it. Any Home Dimension army would have taken one look at it and fired the inventor rather than the mortar.

Its only virtue was that it worked. Blade demonstrated this, firing the mortar by pulling on a long cord from the shelter of a wall of sandbags. The shell flew more than two miles and landed with a puff of dust—a dud. The second shell flew just as far and went off with a tremendous explosion that threw a cloud of dirt and smoke a hundred feet into the air.

"That will probably go right through the roof of any building in Mak'loh," said Blade, after examining the hole in the ground. "If you land one in the middle of a group of androids—"

"Please," said Geetro, wincing at the image, "I can imagine well enough. Do we really need to produce these—monstrosities?"

"Yes," said Sela and Blade, almost together. Blade let the woman go on. "We have to. Otherwise Paron will make them, as soon as he knows they are possible." Blade was silent. He couldn't have put it better himself.

So the mortars and their ammunition went into production, and Blade started training the firing crews and observers. He set up the training range on the far side of the city from Paron's camp and had it heavily patrolled by armed androids. Military security was another thing he was having to reinvent.

Before too long there were five mortars, more than a hundred shells for each one, and a slowly increasing number of trained people. Blade picked out five buildings near the

136

power station and on top of each one put a mortar, its ammunition, and its crew.

Normally everything was kept out of sight, well down inside the spiral ramp from the roof. When Blade gave the signal, the mortar crews would pick up their weapons and shells, rush up to the roof, and be ready to open fire in a minute or two. Blade carefully picked and measured aiming points all around the power plant, to save time in getting the mortars onto their targets.

As Blade said:

"Even if the mortars don't do that much damage, they will certainly be a surprise for Paron. I don't think he's prepared to face one, and that will be half the battle for us."

It was nearly midnight, and everyone in the command post on top of the power plant was asleep except Blade. He himself was leaning back in a folding chair, his feet propped on top of the radio. It had been a long day, starting with seeing two new mortars come out of the factory and go off to the testing range. It was time to call an end to the day and get some sleep.

Blade swung his feet off the radio and stood up. As he stood, the silence of the night suddenly fell apart. Blade recognized the crackle of shock rifles and the crash of grenades. The noise seemed to be coming from the north—toward the area held by Paron.

"Up and alert!" Blade shouted. The people assigned to the command post jerked themselves awake and lurched to their feet. Blade pushed them aside and dashed out onto the roof. He ran to the edge, raised his binoculars, and looked north.

Along half a dozen streets solid masses of moving figures were flowing south. Distance made them ant-like, but the binoculars clearly revealed the red coveralls of soldier androids. A few black dots—humans in Authority coveralls—moved along the fringes of the red masses.

Ahead of them, each street was vanishing under a blanket of silver-gray smoke. As Blade watched, he saw the flash of grenade throwers, and the smoke clouds grew thicker. The front rank of androids seemed to move behind a fringe of

137

white flame, as they fried their rifles continuously into the smoke.

Not a bad plan, thought Blade. Fill the grenades with some sort of chemical compound and use them to lay down a smoke screen. Then blast the area with rifle fire. He doubted Paron could have retrained the androids to kill a clearly visible Master in this short time. He might very well have managed to train them to fire blindly into smoke that *might* hide a Master. That way they could kill a hundred Masters without having to see one of them die or knowing for certain that they'd killed one. That would certainly make the androids a great deal more dangerous during one decisive battle, without making them permanently dangerous.

It also made any effort by Geetro's army to meet the attack in the open streets much too dangerous. Fortunately, they would not have to do anything of the kind—at least not until the mortars had done their work. If they did it.

A woman was bringing the radio out to Blade. He picked it up, switched it on, and punched the General Comman frequency.

"This is Blade. General alert, all hands. Condition Red, Condition Red. Paron is launching a mass android attack from the north. All human and android foot troops, remain in your buildings. Repeat, *remain in your buildings.* All doors should be locked and, if possible, barricaded with furniture.

"Mortar crews, prepare to fire on my command. Good luck, everybody."

Blade picked up his binoculars again. By now the head of each column was vanishing under its smoke screen. The smoke screens themselves were creeping toward Blade down each street.

There was a planned aiming point for the mortars in each of the six streets. There was another in the middle of the square into which all six streets ran. When the mortars opened up. . . .

Blade waited until the head of each column was well past the aiming point in each street. The mortar shells ought to be scattered up and down the column for a considerable distance. Then he picked up the radio.

"Mortar teams—load and sound off."

138

"Team One, loaded and ready!"

"Team Two, all ready!"

Then when all five had called in, Blade took a deep breath.

"All teams—Point 19. Fire on my signal. Five, four, three, two, one, FIRE!"

Five distant thumps came almost together, and then a long silence—mortar shells climb high and quietly. Then suddenly the street farthest to Blade's left spewed flame and smoke. Five shells plunged out of the sky, straight into the column of androids.

Blade did not hear the human and android screams and cries. He could imagine them well enough, for he knew what this kind of heavy fire did to infantry. Not just infantry, but infantry who'd never been trained to meet this kind of attack. None of them knew about mortar fire, and the explosions, the flying fragments, the smoke and the noise would be a nightmarish surprise to both humans and androids.

"Blade to all mortars. "Shift to Point 17." That would bring the shells down on the next column toward the right.

This time four shells were on target, while one plunged through the roof of a building on one side of the street. Even that shell wasn't completely wasted. Blade saw chunks of metal and stone from the roof hurled down on the androids below.

Four more times Blade shifted the fire of the mortars, moving steadily from left to right, hitting each of the six attacking columns in succession. Blade knew that it would be wise to shock and disorganize all six columns rather than wipe out one and leave the other five intact and advancing. Blade guessed Paron's androids outnumbered those of Geetro's army by three or four to one, apart from their new tactics with the smoke screens. Paron could not be allowed to get to close quarters, where those numbers might give him a decisive advantage.

So Blade worked the mortars across all six attacking columns before starting to concentrate on any one. The accuracy of the fire was even better than he'd expected. Authority people in Mak'loh might still have problems with physical activity, but they knew their mathematics forward and backward.

Half the job of hitting the target with any long-range weapon was doing the calculations correctly, so they were off to a good start.

The first salvoes stopped only one of the columns. All six had large chunks blown out of them, and all six were slowed and badly shaken. The smoke screens began to break up as the grenade-throwing androids fell or stopped firing. Instead of the smoke screens, the streets began to vanish in the haze of smoke from the shell explosions.

Blade no longer had to imagine what was happening down there under all the smoke. He could see androids and pieces of androids flying a hundred feet into the air. He could hear extra explosions, as sacks of grenades carried on androids' backs went off. In moments when the smoke eddied, he could see whole sections of street paved from one side to the other with writhing androids. The buildings on either side confined the blast of the explosions and the flying fragments, increasing the effect.

Somehow four of the six attacking columns staggered out into the square. They mingled there like streams flowing into a lake. No one tried to take cover or cross the square. Blade wondered if there were any human beings alive and fit to give the necessary orders.

With grim determination he set out to take advantage of the target the enemy was offering. He ordered all the mortars to hit the square with five rounds apiece. The first salvo came down squarely on target. Before the second one hit, those still alive and on their feet were either running for the side streets or throwing themselves flat. Neither helped very much. The remaining four salvoes walked back and forth across the square. The explosions caught those who were lying flat, blowing them high in the air. Flying fragments caught the runners and cut them down. By the third salvo, smoke from the explosions and from ruptured smoke grenades was spreading across the square, mercifully blotting out what was happening.

A few of the androids were still moving on to the attack, south from the square toward Geetro's perimeter. Blade surveyed them through his binoculars. He counted no more than a hundred. Geetro's humans and androids could sweep them away like a broom. Then it would be time to push north. A determined counterattack could finish off Paron's army for good and win Mak'loh's civil war in a single night. Even if it didn't do that well, it would give Geetro's army the combat experience and the self-confidence it badly needed. Certainly it would do no harm, as long as the mortars kept hammering at Paron's army to keep it from rallying.

Blade was about to order the mortars to bring their shells down along the enemy's line of retreat, when a sudden frantic voice shouted over the radio:

"Blade, Blade! Mortar Four, help! We're being attacked from the air. We're—" The sound of an exploding grenade cut off the voice.

Blade didn't recognize the voice, but a chill hand seemed to be squeezing his stomach. Mortar Four was Sela's assigned battle station.

Sela was half-blinded by the continual sheets of flame from the mortar and more than half-deafened by the roar of the firing. Suddenly the three flyers were there, coming at her out of the darkness.

The mortar crew and the riflemen guarding them were even less aware of the world around them. Sela shouted, but her voice was lost as the mortar fired again. Before she could shout a second time, the flyers swept in over the railing. Rifles flared white from them, half a dozen firing almost together, knocking out the mortar crew and the riflemen.

The flyers landed, close enough that Sela could recognize the man at the controls of one as Paron himself. A man sprang down from Paron's flyer and from the one to the left. Each man pulled a cable with loops and hooks on it after him.

Sela crouched in the shadows, seeing the flyer crews too intent on their business to pay any attention to her. If she kept quiet, they would probably take what they wanted and leave without noticing her.

What they wanted could only be the mortar. Blade said the mortars were the backbone of Geetro's army, and tonight she'd seen how right he was. If Paron got the secret of the mortars. . . .

Sela brought her rifle up in a single, smooth motion, squeezing the trigger as the muzzle came to bear on the men with the cables. The rifle was set to maximum power, and the men went down as if they'd been clubbed, smoking patches of flesh showing on their backs. She was aiming at Paron, when another man whirled in his seat and fired at her.

The beam missed, but it was set to kill, and it came close enough for her to feel it. It was as though someone had pressed white-hot metal wires into her back and neck. It seemed for a moment that her hair itself had taken fire. She screamed, her hands clutching the rifle convulsively, her finger twitching on the trigger, but unable to close on it to shoot Paron out of his seat.

Paron himself turned, saw her, shouted out in incoherent delight, and leaped toward her. He was a stout man who normally moved slowly, but now he seemed to fly toward her as if he'd been shot out of one of the mortars. Sela tried to get to her feet, to meet him with her bare hands if she couldn't fire her rifle. She'd still be able to take him; he was strong but too slow to meet her, he—

Then a grenade went off between two of the flyers, and all the men on or around them went down. Paron cried out, in rage rather than pain. He towered over Sela as she struggled to her knees. He kicked her wildly in the right shoulder, sending her sprawling on her left side. One of Paron's surviving men fired a grenade into the entrance of the downward ramp, and screams followed the explosion.

Paron kicked Sela hard in the stomach, and she doubled up with the world around her fading in a haze of pain. She was aware of him picking her up like a child and heaving her over his shoulder. The movement made her scream, then vomit all over Paron's back.

She knew that he was loading her into the seat of a flyer; then she heard a distant hiss that she recognized as the sound of a spray injector. The last of her knowledge of the world began to slip away. Just before it vanished entirely, she heard the whine of the flyer's fans and felt it stir under her.

Then there was nothing.

Geetro's army stormed out of the buildings where they'd

been waiting. There were five hundred of them, mostly the new recruits from the Houses of Peace, organized in platoons and companies led by Geetro's people from the Authority. The recruits carried rifles, while the officers carried grenade throwers. High above them, Geetro himself rode in a flyer, while from his command post Blade listened in on the radio.

He listened, but he heard very litte, Mak'loh's new soldiers were too busy experiencing the powerfully Physical sensations of their first combat. They had no time to waste telling anybody about it.

One group barricaded themselves so thoroughly that by the time they cleared away all the furniture and broken robots from in front of the door the battle was over. The rest dashed forward. They struck the battered remnants of Paron's columns of androids, and the last stage of the battle exploded through the streets of Mak'loh.

The androids had been slaughtered, confused, and disorganized by the mortar fire. They still would not lie down and die. They could not shoot to kill a clearly visible Master, but they could shoot to stun, and they shot fast and well. The first Physical sensation many of the new recruits felt in combat was being knocked unconscious by android sharpshooters. Some of them felt grenade fragments slicing into their flesh, their own blood flowing, their own internal organs ripped and mangled. Not all of Paron's humans were dead.

In an hour Geetro knew that his human recruits weren't going to win the battle by themselves. He landed his flyer and personally led the reserve of androids into the battle. Slowly they pushed the enemy north, back up the six streets, back to the robot and android plant, back still farther to the wall of the city.

Blade controlled the mortars from his command post until the last of the enemy retreated out of range. Then he went down to the street, climbed into a truck, and rolled forward to join the battle. There was still more than enough battle left for him to join.

The last shots were fired with the eastern sky already turning pink. Daylight came to a battle-scarred city, its streets littered with bodies and wreckage and slimy with human and android blood. In eight hours Mak'loh had known more

143

destruction, more unnatural death, more violent Physical activity, than it had known in the previous eight centuries.

Blade and Geetro met over a hasty breakfast to measure their victory and its cost. There was no doubt about the victory. Twenty of Paron's humans and a few hundred of his androids had fled over the city wall. About as many more had been captured, unharmed or lightly wounded. All the rest were dead or dying. Everything within the city's wall was in Geetro's hands, including all the vital buildings and factories. Some were battered but all still worked.

A hundred of Geetro's humans, and five times as many androids, were dead. Some of the new recruits were whimpering wrecks, their minds temporarily unhinged by the overpowering sensations of combat. The mortars that had decided the battle were practically down to their last shell.

Finally, Sela was gone.

They knew that she'd been alive when Paron put her aboard his flyer and took off. They knew from prisoners that Paron had intended to capture one of the mortars rather than destroy all of them.

"So he seems to be thinking of a long war, where learning our secrets will help him in the end," said Blade. "If he thinks Sela can tell him such secrets, he will not kill her."

"Perhaps not," said Geetro, "but after tonight, will he still believe that he can go on fighting for a long time? What if he knows that he's lost and has nothing left but vegeance? He will certainly take that vengeance on Sela.

"Even if he keeps her alive, it will not be easy for her. If he believes she know our secrets, he will stop at nothing to get them from her. We must go after her, Blade. We must go after Sela and get her back or at least know—" he choked, "—know that she is dead."

Blade considered the matter. After the night's battle, the Inward Eye had lost some of its appeal in Mak'loh. People were pouring out of the Houses of Peace by the hundred, rallying to Geetro.

Some of them were intelligent enough to realize that in this crisis everyone had to wake up and get to work. Most of them still had no interest in anything but new, more exhilarating, sensations. They'd heard that joining Geetro's army offered the best opportunity around for such sensations. There were enough potential volunteers for the army to replace last night's losses twenty times over.

There was also a great deal of damage in the city that should be repaired. It would have been much better to put these enthusiasts to work there. Unfortunately, most of them didn't know one end of a tool from the other. They would be useless or even dangerous. In the army, they might be useful once they were trained—not for serious fighting, of course— but with Paron defeated, there was no danger of that for some time.

What better way to train the new army then to send it out to search all the land of Mak'loh as far as the outer Wall? They could search out Paron's fugitives and Sela, if she were still alive. It was a job that would have to be done sooner or later, and probably the sooner the better.

"Certainly," said Blade, "let's get the new recruits organized a bit and send them out. They'll need officers, so I suggest we pick out the best of last night's veterans and put them in charge." He rose, and Geetro rose to follow him.

Chapter 19

Sela awoke to feel sharp pains in a good many places she hadn't expected them. She vaguely wondered if Paron's flyer had crashed and she was now pinned in the wreckage, dying. She hoped that death would come quickly. After a little while, she drifted off into darkness again, wondering if she were dying, but hardly caring.

When she awoke a second time, the pains had faded and she was aware of other things as well. Her hands and feet were tightly bound with cords. A bed of cut branches was under her. Above her she could see the branches of trees, with the sun shining through the leaves. A breeze blew over her, smelling of flowers and stagnant water and bringing the faint hum of insects with it. Suddenly there was Paron's heavy face as well, peering down into hers.

He squatted and clamped one hand around her chin to force her head toward him. The movement hurt. He saw the pain in her face and smiled. "I will hurt you far more if you do not tell me all the things I need to know. Think of that, Sela."

He seemed to expect some reply to that statement.

Slowly she shook her head. "I cannot tell you anything."

He slapped her hard, three times. Her eyes watered, and she tasted blood from a cut lip. She forced herself to speak calmly and coldly.

"The more you strike me, the less I will tell you. If you go on threatening me, you will learn nothing at all while I live. After I am dead, what can I tell you?"

Paron's fingers were obviously itching to slap her again, or do something even more painful. Her tone stopped him. In

147

his eyes she could see a wild desire to inflict pain fighting against an equally powerful desire to learn all he could about his enemies.

"That is true," he said finally. "I will not kill you. Not now, perhaps not at all. Perhaps when I have taken Mak'loh back and rule it, you can rule beside me. If you prove yourself worthy, this can be. But you cannot rule Mak'loh beside me if I do not take it back, can you?"

"I suppose not."

"Then you have to tell me what I need to know to get it back. You *have to!*" The last two words were almost a scream. They made Sela shiver and nearly lose her pose of calm. She had no doubt that sooner or later Paron would torture or kill her if she didn't tell him what he wanted to know. She also had no doubt that beyond a certain point she would probably break down and tell him. Paron had done a good deal of research into the systematic infliction of pain, practicing on androids. She would be subjected to tortures that might destroy her mind before they destroyed her body, unless she betrayed Blade and Geetro.

Or until she could deceive Paron, leading him on, gaining time. Time to see what Paron might be planning to do. Time to judge her chances of escape. Time to think about putting an end to her own life before the torture began, if she could find no way of escaping.

She took a deep breath. "Paron, listen! I cannot tell you anything until I know what you want to know. Surely you are not interested in when Blade and Geetro go to relieve themselves, are you?"

He laughed, showing all his teeth, but no real amusement. "I am not. Very well. I shall tell you more." He took a knife from his belt and bent down to cut her bonds.

Suddenly Paron whirled around, as branches rustled behind him. The head of an android appeared over the top of a bush. "Master, it begins—"

Paron whirled to face the android. One thick arm shot out and gripped the android by the collar, pulling it headfirst through the bush. As the android twisted and squalled in wordless protest, Paron's other hand thrust the knife into its throat. The android died, bubbling and gasping and spraying blood all over the little clearing and all over Paron and Sela.

It took all her self-control to keep from screaming. Paron was mad. He killed for the love of killing, and she was absolutely in his power.

At that thought she no longer felt like screaming. She felt more like vomiting, except that her stomach was too empty.

Over the next several days, Sela gradually realized that her situation was not as bad as she'd thought. She couldn't really call herself safe until Paron was dead or she was out of his reach. Paron could still kill her as easily as swatting a fly. But he no longer had the strength to do much damage to Mak'loh.

He took her everywhere in his little camp in the forest and showed her everything until she was able to measure his strength. He had a single flyer. He had fewer than two hundred soldier androids, about as many workers, and a hundred assorted robots. He had no more than twenty humans, and several of these were wounded or helpless, drooling idiots, even madder than Paron. He had little ammunition and less equipment. He had practically no food, and he was trying to feed his humans on fruits and nuts from the forest around them. The usual diet gave Sela continuous stomach cramps, but she was luckier than one man. He died screaming and vomiting blood, victim of something poisonous.

Paron was finished. It didn't matter whether he realized this or not. Nor did it matter if Sela freely told him everything she knew about Blade's plans. It would be impossible for him to do anything with that knowledge. All she had to do was to wait until Blade and Geetro led their soldiers out to clear the land of Mak'loh.

Wait, and in the meantime stay alive. She was slow and cautious in answering Paron, asking him three questions for every one he asked her. She wanted to be absolutely sure of giving him everything he needed, or so she told him. Actually, she suspected that he might kill or torture her for his own amusement when he thought she'd told him everything. So she would take as long as possible.

Fortunately for Sela, Paron seemed as interested in talking

149

as in listening. He told wild tales of what he would do to his enemies when he ruled in Mak'loh. He told even wilder tales of the invincible secret weapons he would develop when he had the factories of Mak'loh at his command again. He even spoke of his dream of launching a war against all the other Cities of Peace.

"It is certain that we cannot trust them, if they produce men like Blade. Where there is one man like him, there may be thousands. They will certainly try to destroy us. The only way we can prevent this is to destroy them first. Mak'loh must rule for a thousand years before it is safe. I shall rule Mak'loh, and you shall help me!"

At times it was almost impossible for Sela to listen to Paron's ravings with a straight face. Paron had a better imagination than anyone who had ever made up an Inward Eye tape! But then, all the Inward Eye tapes had been made by people who hadn't lost their wits.

If Paron had been talking about anything that he had some hope of doing, Sela would have listened more carefully. Any knowledge of the enemy's plans would be useful to Blade and Geetro. Since Paron was making no more sense than the birds or the squirrels, she didn't think Blade and Geetro would be at all interested.

Sela quickly realized that escaping would not be as easy as she'd hoped, in spite of the pitifully small size of Paron's army. For several days he would not even let her out of his private camp. The walls of the camp were eight feet high, built of solid logs and topped with thorn branches. It was patrolled both inside and outside by armed androids.

When Paron finally did let her out into the forest, he either went with her himself or sent a guard of at least six armed androids. To be sure, the androids knew she was a Master. They would not kill her—but they would certainly stun her on the spot for any attempt to escape, then turn her over to Paron. What he would do then, she didn't care to think about, and still less cared to risk.

If Blade and Geetro were to find the camp—unfortunately, that wasn't likely. The forest would make the camp almost invisible from the air, and it would take a long time to search the city's land tree by tree.

It was a race between Paron's madness, her own escape, and Blade's searching parties. Who would win?

The water of the stream was dark, but clean and cold. Sela swam up and down as far as the android guards would allow her, letting the water clean the dirt off her body and for the moment clean the worries out of her mind. It was two weeks since she'd been captured, and she was no closer to a way to escape than the day she'd arrived. So far Paron seemed to have no desire to kill her. He'd killed several androids and raped one woman when she complained of the wretched food, but he hadn't laid a finger on Sela. How long would her luck hold?

She turned over on her back and swam upstream with slow, steady strokes. On the bank two androids gazed down at her. She found this bothered her and was surprised to feel that way. Before Blade came, she had never worried about being naked in the presence of androids. Now she felt she would like to do almost anything herself rather than have androids underfoot all the time to wait on her. She wondered how many other people in Mak'loh might be feeling the same way. "The city of the living dead," Blade had called Mak'loh. Well, perhaps the dead were coming back to real life.

She laughed softly. Then the branches on the bank between the two androids parted, and her laugh died as three men sprang out into the open. They seemed to explode out of the bushes, and the sunlight blazed from the swords in their hands. Two swang at the androids on either side of them. One android's head flew off its shoulders, the other's face opened in a great ragged gash.

The other four androids of Sela's escort were on the other bank of the stream. They raised their rifles as the third attacker raised a long metal tube. The rifles flared white, and the tube gushed orange flame and dirty white smoke. One of the androids fell over backward, hands clutched to his stomach. Two of the three swordsmen fell, struck down by the rifle fire. The third sprang back into the bushes as suddenly as he'd appeared.

Sela reached up onto the bank and snatched up a rifle dropped by one of the maimed androids. Before the surviving androids realized what she was doing, she shot all three of them. Two sprawled on the bank; the third fell with a splash into the stream. Sela grabbed a root with one hand and heaved herself out of the water.

Without bothering to dress, she plunged into the bushes, ignoring the branches that lashed across her bare skin. She knew who those swordsmen were. From Blade's description, she recognized them as the soldiers of the Warland ruler, the Shoba.

She knew who they were. *How had they entered Mak'loh?* The question screamed itself in her mind, and she wanted to scream it out loud. She forced herself to keep silent. She had to get away from the Shoba's men and bring warning of their attack to the city. That meant getting to Paron's flyer. If she failed. . . .

If she failed, the Shoba's men might swarm across the land of Mak'loh and arrive at the city's wall before anyone knew they were coming. What would happen then, she asked herself? She remembered what Blade had said once about the soldiers of the Shoba.

"If they come to Mak'loh, they will be deadly enemies. We have stronger weapons, but theirs are not weak. They are also brave men, and far more skilled in many kinds of fighting than our people or even the soldier androids. A battle against the Shoba could be Mak'loh's last battle."

Sela remembered that the weapons of the Shoba's men could not hit a moving target as well as the shock rifles of Mak'loh. So she ran as fast as the bushes and the ground underfoot would let her, although her legs and feet began to ooze blood from thorn scratches and sharp roots.

She plunged between two trees and came out into a small clearing. Three worker androids were running across it. Two of the Shoba's men were on their heels, waving swords that already dripped with silver-tinged android blood.

Sela let the androids pass and fired at the first swordsman. He went down in midstride, sliding several yards on his face. Before she could aim at the second man, he swung his sword. It caught her rifle with savage force, knocking it out of her tingling hands. The swordsman raised his weapon, ready to take her head off or lay her stomach open. Then he realized that he faced an unarmed, naked, lovely woman. Lust flared in his eyes, and the sword wavered for a moment.

That was all the time Sela needed. She closed and leaped high, driving one foot in past the man's sword to smash into his chest. The metal rings of his armor bruised and gouged her foot, but the man went down. Sela landed, whirled, and stamped her other foot down on the man's upturned face. He screamed and clawed at his smashed nose and teeth. Sela snatched up her rifle and darted across the clearing into cover again.

Sometimes running, sometimes walking, sometimes crawling on her belly like an animal, Sela crossed the camp area toward the flyer. There were soldiers of the Shoba all over the place. Many of them were dead or dying, but far too many were alive and on the prowl. However they had crossed the Wall, they had done so in force, and they had certainly won their first battle.

There was no doubt of that. All the androids Sela found were dead or crippled. Their armored vests would keep an arrow or a musket ball from penetrating, but not from knocking them down. Once they were down, the Shoba's men would close in firing at the android's heads, hacking or thrusting at their arms and legs. Sela found several androids dying slowly in whimpering agony and used nerve pinches to give them a silent and merciful death.

She saw other ugly sights too and had to slip by without doing anything about them. A man pinned to a large tree by knives driven through his hands, while the soldiers shot at him with arrows. A woman spread-eagled naked on the grass, while a soldier hammered himself into her and thirty more waited their turn. Sela's stomach churned at the thought of this sort of thing happening in every street of Mak'loh.

The last body Sela found before reaching the flyer was Paron himself. Mad as he was, he'd died fighting. Six of the Shoba's men lay dead around him, and his hands were locked tight on the throat of a seventh. His body a mass of gashes and bullet holes where it didn't bristle with arrows.

Paron was dead and the last danger to Mak'loh from him gone forever. In his place, a new and far worse danger had sprung up. Paron would at least have preserved much of the city's knowledge and therefore much of its future. The Shoba's soldiers would only kill, loot, and destroy.

The flyer lay on the near side of a wide clearing. Sela peered through the trees and sighed with relief. There were none of the Shoba's men in sight, and the machine itself appeared to be completely intact. Perhaps the enemy hadn't come this far. She ran forward, out into the clearing.

As she did, several enemy soldiers emerged from the trees on the far side of the clearing. Sela leaped for the flyer, at the same time aiming her rifle. The soldiers grabbed arrows, and both sides let fly at the same time.

Sela's aim was good, but the range was too great for the beam of her rifle. The white fire crackled out of existence, well short of the unharmed soldiers. She screamed in frustration, then screamed in pain as one of the plunging arrows sliced into her thigh. She dropped the rifle, heaved herself into the seat of the flyer, and started the fans. More arrows whistled down about her, but this time all of them missed. Before the archers could fire a third time, the flyer was lifting off the grass. It shot straight up, hitting an overhanging branch so hard that Sela nearly lost control. Then she was climbing up and away.

She kept climbing until she was certain that nothing from the ground could hit her. She climbed even farther, until she could see the towers of Mak'loh in the distance. She firmly put out of her mind the arrow in her thigh, the pain it was causing, and everything else except reaching those towers. Then she set course for the city, as fast as the flyer would go.

Chapter 20

It was impossible to keep secret Sela's arrival, wearing nothing but an arrow in her thigh and the blood of her victims. Rumors ran around the streets of Mak'loh, and after the rumors came panic. Even many of Geetro's old supporters seemed confused and uncertain, while those who had only left the Houses of Peace a few days before were half out of their minds with fear.

The moment he was sure Sela was in no danger, Blade took off in a flyer and headed toward where Paron's camp had been. This lay well off to the north of the city, along a stretch of the outer Wall invisible from the Warlands plains below. It was just possible that the Shoba was only launching a raid, or even an exploring party. It wasn't likely. The Shoba's commanders had been intelligent enough to notice that the Wall was no longer defended by the various force fields. They would almost certainly be intelligent enough to realize this situation might not last forever. An attack over the Wall would have to be delivered with all the strength at their command, trying for a single knockout punch. They would not risk throwing away the advantage of surprise by making small raids.

Before nightfall Blade returned to Mak'loh, knowing he'd guessed right. From the air he'd been able to see the Shoba's whole army spread out below him—at least forty thousand men and more than a hundred guns.

From the air Blade could see that a narrow valley led west, along the northern Wall of Mak'loh. Ten miles up the valley was a place where the Wall stood on top of a gentle slope—

gentle enough for drun cavalry, artillery, and even supply wagons, as well as infantry.

With the force fields down, it had been easy enough to approach the Wall, send scouts over it, then blow three great gaps with gunpowder. Now the Shoba's army was marching in an endless stream through those gaps. Ahead of it went a screen of mounted archers and working parties to chop a road through the forest.

Where were the Watchers? Blade saw many of them lying smashed on the ground along the Wall. A few were surrounded by a ring of corpses. Some had fought and given a good account of themselves. Apparently most simply couldn't react correctly without the warning of the Entesh Field and with their programming so unreliable. They'd attacked hesitantly and piecemeal, and been smashed by musket fire. A Watcher would be a target that even a black-powder matchlock could hardly miss. They'd gone down, and without noticeably weakening the Shoba's army.

Whatever happened in the next few days or weeks, the people of Mak'loh would have to start patrolling their own Walls. That would be an enormous step in the right direction—if the people lived long enough to take it.

It was quite possible they wouldn't. Blade summarized the situation for Geetro and Sela after his return that night.

"We can't hope for more than five or six thousand people from the Houses of Peace who will be any good in a fight. We have ten thousand soldier androids. We have rifles for all of these, and a few hundred grenade throwers. We are short of both power cells and grenades. We. . . ."

"We are making more of both, and quickly," said Geetro. "We will not be short for long."

"That is true, if the Shoba's men go away quickly," said Blade. "But consider this, Geetro. We are using more grenades and cartridges this one year than have been used in the past thousand. The supply of material to make them is not so great, and we must go outside the Wall to get more. What if the Shoba's men tighten their ring around the city until we cannot leave it?"

"I have thought of that," said Geetro. "There is much metal and other material in the Houses of Peace. Some of my people are calculating how to turn it into weapons. They have discovered, for example, that in a single Inward Eye machine there is enough metal to make a hundred grenades or a mortar. As for the explosives—"

Blade held up a hand, although he badly wanted to hear more. He had to force himself not to grin in triumph. Turning Inward Eye machines into weapons would be another enormous step away from the old way of life.

Unfortunately, it would also take time, which Mak'loh might not have. Blade continued.

"We have twelve mortars, people to fire them, and much ammunition. The mortars should be kept out of sight and not used unless the Shoba's men are actually climbing over the city's wall. We want to keep the mortars as a surprise for the Shoba, as they were for Paron."

Neither Geetro nor Sela needed to be convinced on that point.

"There is much we can do with what we have, but it will not be enough. As Sela knows too well, the Shoba's archers can shoot farther than our rifles. Their cannon can shoot even farther than that. We do not have enough grenade throwers or mortars to fight a battle only with those weapons."

"Do the Shoba's men know about our rifles and their bows?" said Geetro.

"They will soon enough," said Blade. "Then they may send their archers up to the city's wall, to shoot at our riflemen. When the riflemen are dead, other soldiers can run up to the wall and climb it on ladders or ropes. Or they can dig a tunnel in the earth, put powder under the wall, and blow a hole in it. Or—" He shrugged. "There are too many things they can do, if we give them time. The Shoba's men not only fight well, they see clearly and think quickly.

"So we cannot wait behind the walls of Mak'loh until they attack. We must be able to go out and meet them in battle and defeat them. For that we need the help of the people of the villages in the Warlands."

Both Geetro and Sela were too polite, or perhaps too desperate, to tell Blade to his face that he'd gone mad, but both looked skeptical. "If the Shoba's soldiers are as good as you say they are, what can the Warlands villagers do against them?" asked Geetro. "The villagers were wretched barbarians the last time we fought them. Do you know that they are better now?"

"I do." Swiftly Blade outlined his plan. Some of it was pure bluff, and some of it was educated guesswork. Much of it, though, was what he'd seen in the Warlands or learned from Twana. Irony—Twana was dead, but what she'd told Blade might lead to a great victory for both Mak'loh and for her own people. She would deserve a large place in the history books of this Dimension, although she'd probably never get it.

He finished, "If the villages of the Warlands can send seven thousand fighting men, we can carry out this plan. Even with five thousand, I might be prepared to risk it.

"So I will go to the Warland villages, in a flyer. I will start at Hores, Twana's village, where her father, Naran, is the chief. He is said to be a brave and wise man, who will understand what must be done. If he joins us and speaks for us in the other villages, we will have less trouble. So I will leave tonight, and—"

"No, Blade," said Sela. "I will go with you. It is necessary." Both Geetro and Blade stared at her, but she ignored them. "There must be someone from Mak'loh, who can speak for the Authority. You. . . ."

"Sela!" exploded Geetro. "You have just escaped from Paron, and you are wounded as well. You cannot go with Blade!"

"I cannot walk for many days and nights; that is true," said Sela. "But I can certainly ride in a flyer and speak to village chiefs. Geetro, you have work to do here. You must get the city ready to defend itself until the Warlanders come. That is work I cannot do. Please, Geetro."

There was a pleading look in her eyes and a pleading note in her voice, both so strong that Geetro finally yielded. "Very well, Sela. Go with Blade, and bring back the Warlanders. But if you don't get her back safely, Blade, I swear I'll kill you with my bare hands!" His tone made it clear that he was not joking.

"She'll be on her way back as soon as the talking is over,"

said Blade. "I swear this." The two men shook hands, and Blade decided to leave Geetro alone with Sela.

As he went out the door, he heard Geetro's voice. "I think we'd better have the worker androids block off a square in the heart of the city. We must have some area we can still defend, even if they do get over the wall.

"Also, I think we should put some of the mortars on the trucks, so they can be moved—"

Blade closed the door behind him and went off down the corridor with a smile on his face. Geetro was a man who would go far and fast once you gave him a slight shove in the right direction. Blade hoped there were more like Geetro in Mak'loh.

Blade and Sela took off the next morning, just after the lookouts on the walls sighted the first of the Shoba's scouts. Blade took the flyer up to a safe altitude and headed straight toward the east.

They were over the Wall in half an hour, and Blade turned north toward Hores. He only hoped it was still standing. He doubted if the Shoba's army had been able to spend much time or effort scouring the countryside beyond the Wall. Hores, though, lay not far from the army's line of march. They might have reduced it to smoldering ruins just to protect their flank.

A few miles south of Hores, Blade dropped down to low altitude to avoid being spotted by either friend or enemy. He swung wide to the east and came in over the same orchard from which he'd watched Twana's kidnapping.

The village stood exactly as it had been, completely intact. There seemed to be even more people than he remembered at work in the fields and passing in and out of the gate. All of them froze as Blade's flyer sailed over the trees and hovered in front of the gate. As he landed, some people ran, others dropped flat as if he'd turned a shock rifle on them, and a few grabbed bows and spears. None of them seemed ready to go into action, but none of them seemed quite ready to be friendly, either. Blade and Sela obviously weren't part of the Shoba's army, but they were something even stranger, and perhaps just as dangerous.

Blade stepped down to the ground, hands held out in the classic gesture of peace. "I have important words to speak to Naran, your chief," he said. "Bring me to him."

"What words?" said several people almost together. "Who are you? Why do you come to us?" Someone added, "Do you serve the Shoba?" and drew his bow taut. Blade hoped Sela would keep her hands off her rifle. It might not take much to provoke a shooting match, fatal not only to the two of them but to Mak'loh's chances of an alliance with the Warlanders.

"I am from beyond the Wall," he said in a level voice. "I do not serve the Shoba. I hate him as much as you do. His soldiers have crossed the Wall and are making war against the city there. It is called Mak'loh. If it falls, the Shoba's army will turn on you next. If you come to the aid of Mak'loh, the Shoba's army will be destroyed, and Mak'loh will—"

At this point Blade broke off, because it was obvious that the people were no longer listening to a word he was saying. They were staring at each other as if they weren't sure who was mad—Blade or them—or even if Blade were real. Then someone muttered something, out of which Blade caught only the single word "Naran," and somebody else sprinted for the village gate.

Blade stood in the middle of the circle of archers and spearmen, while the sweat began to trickle down his face and a fly settled on his nose. He didn't dare even to raise a hand to brush it off.

Then the messenger came back, and behind him the same man Blade had seen beaten and kicked by the Shoba's soldiers. The chief looked ten years older and walked with a cane, but his eyes were still sharp as they fell on Blade.

Blade turned slowly and raised both hands in salute to the chief.

"Hail, Naran, I come from beyond the Wall, to bring you news of the city of Mak'loh, of the army of the Shoba, and of your daughter Twana."

Naran had too much dignity and self-control to start at Blade's words, but his eyes opened very wide and it was a moment before he spoke. Then he said slowly, "Come with me, Blade of Mak'loh. I think we should speak together."

160

The "speaking together" took longer than Blade had expected. This was not because Naran was slowwitted or argumentative. It was because Blade and Sela had to explain the situation and propose the alliance three separate times. The first time they spoke with Naran alone. The second time they spoke with Naran and the subchiefs oft he village of Hores. The third time they spoke with Naran and the chiefs and war leaders of a dozen other villages, whose fighting men were already in Naran's village or camped within a day's march of it.

The Shoba's army had originally come into the area to punish the villages for their "rebellion"—meaning Blade's attacks and Twana's escape. The villagers suspected this from the first and quickly confirmed it from a few captured scouts. They knew well enough what an army this size could do to them and how little they could do against it.

Yet they'd made up their minds to resist as well as they could. Some four thousand fighting men had been gathered from all the villages within three days' march of Hores. They had been assembled here in the north, to harry and ambush the Shoba's men as they moved south along the Wall. If nothing else, they could perhaps kill the sniffers and so make it possible for the people of the villages farther south to flee and hide themselves.

In fact, they'd all expected to be dead by now. Instead, the Shoba's army suddenly marched off into the hills and vanished as completely as if it had marched off the edge of the world. There were some in the villages who said they thought they'd seen something possibly happening to the Wall, but as Naran said:

"This told us no more than the humming of the dragonflies over a pond in the evening."

No one quite dared to suggest that the Shoba's army was marching against the Wall. "Yet many of us began to think strange thoughts," said Naran. "Something was drawing the Shoba's men away from us. Even in the time of our remotest ancestors, there were legends of life beyond the Wall. So we have been ready to believe what you came to tell us. We have even made the fighting men of the villages ready to be led against the Shoba."

161

Blade smiled. "I wish I could lead them straight over the Wall tomorrow morning. But those you have here are not enough. Also, it would be wiser to cross the Wall farther to the south. That way we shall reach Mak'loh more swiftly and give the Shoba a great surprise."

Naran frowned. "Then the help of other villages will be needed?"

"Yes. However brave the four thousand you have here might be, they would be going to their deaths."

"Very well then. It will be necessary to travel about among the other villages and speak to their chiefs. Will you carry me in your flying machine?"

Both Blade and Sela stared at the old man. Their surprise seemed to amuse him. "Why not?" he said. "I am too old to walk all the way, even if we had the time. Your machine is strange, but not, I think, evil. That no man of Hores has ever ridden in one before does not worry me."

He sighed. "I had thought the old ways of our village would go on, into the time of my children's children's children. Now I can see that they will not even go on to the end of my own time, whether I wish it or not. Certainly no one in any of the villages will be unhappy if we no longer have to stand alone against the Shoba."

Blade, Sela, and Naran spent the next several days flying from village to village, calling on them to send out their fighting men to aid Mak'loh against the Shoba. Nearly all the chiefs and war leaders were more than willing, provided that Mak'loh would feed them and also give them some of its powerful fire-throwers.

Food would be no problem—the food factories could produce enough for an army ten times larger than the villages could send. Blade had his doubts about handing out the shock rifles, but Sela was enthusiastic. In several villages she made the suggestion without even being asked.

Village after village promised their men, until Blade knew that he would have at least ten thousand and probably many more. All that remained was to gather the Warlands army and pass it through the Wall. Naran would give all the orders needed for the first job, and Blade and Sela quickly made the necessary arrangements for the second one.

The night before they were to fly to join the army, Blade and Sela sat in a hut in Hores. Between them on the floor lay the remains of a roasted goat, a jug of beer, and two tallow candles that cast a flickering light around the low room.

Blade poured more beer into the cups, and they drank a toast to the future of Mak'loh and its allies and the doom of the Shoba. Then Blade asked, "Sela—why have you been so free offering shock rifles to these people? I know the rifles are easy to use, but have you no fear they may be used against Mak'loh in time?"

"Perhaps," said Sela. "But if the Warlanders turn the rifles against us, we need only stop giving them the power cells. Then the rifles will be useless. Meanwhile, they will no longer be in Mak'loh. Thus Geetro will have the excuse he wants, to give out those rifles which remain in the city only to those people he trusts."

Blade nodded politely without saying anything. So Geetro was thinking of setting himself up as dictator—or at least strongman—of the new Mak'loh? Well, Mak'loh was reviving every other part of civilization, so they might as well revive politics! Certainly he could hardly expect to do anything about it in whatever time he had left in this Dimension.

Before he could think anymore along those lines, Sela rose painfully to her feet. She undid the coarse wool robe that was her only garment and let it slip to the floor. The candlelight sent gleams up and down her body as she took Blade's hand and led him to the pile of furs in the corner.

As they lay together afterward, Sela gave a long, luxurious sigh and said, with her mouth half-muffled against his chest, "This must be the last time for us."

"Geetro?" said Blade.

"Yes. He and I will do well together, I think. He has many of your qualities, and he is also of Mak'loh. You are of England, and sooner or later you will be going back there."

"That is true," said Blade. "I'm glad you've seen this without my having to tell you." Unseen in darkness, he smiled. Were any of Geetro's qualities as important to Sela as his probably being the next ruler of Mak'loh? Blade wondered.

Well, Geetro might end up ruling Mak'loh, but Sela would

very likely rule Geetro. The city and its people could do much worse.

Blade stood at the bottom of the hill and watched the flyer swooping low over the Wall. Sela was at the controls of the flyer, and at a radio signal from her the explosives placed under a section of the Wall would be detonated. The way into Mak'loh would be open for the army of the Warland villages.

Blade turned and looked at the fighting men of the villages, twelve thousand of them drawn up and ready to march. They carried spears, swords, bows, and axes. The two thousand shock rifles they'd been promised would be handed out when they reached Mak'loh.

As Blade turned, the sun glinted from a massive collar he wore around his neck, over his faded black Authority coveralls. Each piece of the collar was a bar of gold weighing nearly a pound, and Blade felt that it would crumble his collarbone into powder if he had to wear it much longer.

It was the War Collar of a High Chief of all the villages. Blade smiled as he remembered what Naran had said as he fastened the collar around Blade's neck.

"We have seldom needed a High Chief, we don't really need one now, and we probably won't need one after all this is over. If we do need one, you'll have to give the collar back. Meanwhile, though, you're doing what a High Chief is chosen to do—leading all the villages into a great war. So we might as well give you the collar." Then he lowered his voice and spoke so that only Blade could hear, "I do this also out of gratitude for what you did for Twana."

Blade looked up at the hill, raised his rifle, and fired into the air three times. Sela's flyer climbed away from the Wall, until it circled above the Warlanders. The radio signal flashed down from it, and suddenly half a mile of Wall vanished in gray smoke.

Seconds later the roar of the explosion reached Blade's ears, and the ground began to shiver under his feet. The roar and the shivering built steadily, and the smoke billowed higher and higher, as if the earth were catching fire. In the grayness Blade saw darker chunks, first rising and then falling—bits of the wall hurled into the air.

At last the smoke began to drift away, and Blade saw more bits of the Wall rolling down the hill toward him. Long before they reached him, the last of the smoke was gone. Along the whole half mile the Wall was crumbling into dust and gravel. Behind him Blade could hear the swelling cheers of the Warlanders.

In throwing Mak'loh open to its new allies, Geetro had certainly chosen to make a grand gesture!

Chapter 21

The march of the Warland villagers started off with a literal bang, but rapidly became a first-class headache for Richard Blade. The villagers had great enthusiasm and great endurance, but they had no real discipline. They straggled behind, they ran on ahead, they made camp when and where they pleased, they built fires until Blade was sure the smoke would warn the Shoba's army. None of the men would willingly follow the orders of any chief but his own, and none of the chiefs would take orders from anybody at all except Blade and Naran. Blade was certain these people would be brave enough on the battlefield—if he could get them that far without throttling half of them in sheer frustration. He was not at all sure if that courage would be enough against the disciplined advance and firepower of the Shoba's infantry or the hammering charges of his cavalry.

The villagers could not really hope to face the Shoba's army in the open field. Neither could the people and androids of Mak'loh, not when the Shoba's archers could outrange the shock rifles. How could they avoid such a battle, though, unless the Shoba's men could be baited into an attack on the city itself?

Blade's beard grew longer and his temper grew shorter as he led the twelve thousand villagers in a wide swing to the south. They came up on the opposite side of the city from the Shoba's army and made camp under cover of the forest beyond the range of the enemy's scouts. It was five days since they'd passed through the breach in the Wall.

Luck was on their side. The Shoba's commanders knew their business well—too well to risk dispersing their forces in the face of an enemy whose powers had not yet been fully revealed. So they set up a vast, fortified camp three miles from the northern edge of the city. That was well beyond the range of the mortars, and Blade wondered at first if the enemy had guessed Mak'loh's secret weapon. A quick flight over the camp set his doubts to rest. The camp site had been chosen because it lay between two streams, and therefore had plenty of fresh water.

The camp was a formidable thing, a square over a mile on a side. It was surrounded by a protective ditch, high earth embankments, and a palisade of sharpened logs on top of the embankment. It would take the mortars to do much against the camp, but to get within range they would have to be brought out of the city. In that case they'd have to be protected, and protecting them against the Shoba's army would take every man the city and the villagers had between them. Otherwise, the mortars would be quickly overrun, and with them would go Mak'loh's best chance of victory.

It would have to be a battle in the open field, however unsuited this weirdly assorted army Blade led might be for such a battle. He resigned himself to this fact and set about planning the best tactics.

The Shoba's army kept a close watch on the northern wall of the city. In fact, they cleared all the ground between their camp and the city until nothing larger than a rabbit could get in or out without being noticed. On the other three sides of the city, they kept watch with nothing more than occasional cavalry patrols. They seemed to be waiting for Mak'loh to show its hand.

Blade would be happy to let them wait as long as they pleased. The night after the Warlands army made camp, a convoy of trucks rolled out of a gate in the south wall of the city. It brought to the camp a month's food and the promised two thousand shock rifles, then returned before dawn brought the enemy's patrols. Doubtless the drun-riders saw the wheel tracks, but could not follow them up. Druns were stronger than horses and faster on level ground, but much less surefooted. As long as the villagers were shielded by the forest, they'd be safe from detection.

A number of Geetro's people came out in the convoy to

instruct the villagers in using the rifles. Blade gave them their orders, then flew back into the city, and sat down with Geetro and Sela to make their plans for the battle.

Mak'loh had a number of assets that could give it a resounding victory if they were properly used. There were the mortars. There were the six-wheeled trucks. There were the robots—the last few Watchers and all the work models. There were the thousands upon thousands of worker androids. They could build or tear down anything that might be needed for any plans Blade might make. Finally, there was the wall around the city. Blade had often cursed it, for Twana had died there. Now he was grateful for it. It kept the Shoba's men out of the streets of Mak'loh and completely concealed from them anything that might go on there. The androids patrolled it too well for anyone to climb it. The Shoba's men could only stare at it from a distance and wonder who and what lay behind it.

Dawn, and Blade was climbing up through the branches of a tree on the edge of the forest nearest the enemy's camp. The leaves were still damp.

He found a high branch that would bear his weight and crawled out on it. The camp was already coming awake in the gray light, with drums and trumpets, smoke curling up from cook fires, and the clink of armor and thud of feet as the night guard marched in and the morning guard marched out. Both lines of men marched with the snap and precision Blade had always seen in the Shoba's men. Their discipline and training were unbroken.

Surrounded by their own palisade, three wooden siege towers rose to the left of the camp. Each tower stood fifty feet high and was mounted on solid wheels that were sections of whole trees. Three more were under construction. All six would soon be spearheading an assault on the walls of Mak'loh. They would be virtually invulnerable to the shock rifles or to any weapon the Warlanders carried. As Blade had expected, it wasn't safe to leave the initiative to the Shoba's soldiers. They could do too much with it. An army like that had to be confronted with an attack so violent and so sudden that it simply couldn't react fast enough.

169

Behind him under cover of the forest lay the twelve thousand fighting men of the Warlands villages. They were stripped to weapons and loinguards for speed and ease of movement. Their chiefs walked among them now, promising death to any man who held back or who spoke above a whisper before the High Chief Blade gave the signal. They needed surprise.

Beyond the camp, the rising sun was beginning to strike fire from the high towers of Mak'loh. Blade had lived among them for so long that he'd forgotten their beauty. Now he was more aware of that beauty than ever before, with the heightened awareness that sometimes came to him as he waited for battle.

He'd have to wait for quite a while this morning. Sela and Geetro had to make the first move.

Sela stood at the head of her company and looked behind her. Three thousand humans and six thousand soldier androids were drawn up in lines by the city wall. Around them on the other three sides rose lower walls, built from demolished buildings by the hordes of worker androids. Anyone coming in through the new gates in the city wall would find himself boxed in by these walls. He would then find himself under fire from android riflemen and even the mortars.

Sela hoped the mortars wouldn't be needed to hold the city today. They could do so much more in the battle in the open that was now less than half an hour away. Much depended on how fast the Shoba's men responded to Mak'loh's challenge, of course. Blade thought they wouldn't resist a chance to crush a weaker foe, and Sela hoped he was right.

Sela raised her hand and signalled. Three sharp explosions sounded from the city wall. The metal plates that disguised both sides of the new gates tottered and fell, inward and outward. Sela looked through the center gate to see green grass rolling away toward the distant sprawling mass of the enemy's camp.

Then she raised her hand again, fired her rifle into the air, and led her people toward the gateways.

Sela's humans and androids came out of the gates faster

170

than Blade had dared hope. There would be no danger of the Shoba's army launching a quick attack in the hope of catching their enemy divided and unformed. Good. Such an attack might not win the battle for the Shoba, but it would certainly make it far more costly for Mak'loh. It would probably mean Sela's death, at the very least.

Before the Shoba's soldiers realized what was going on, nearly all of Sela's army was out of the city. Then the trumpets and drums began to sound, building into a steady din that was almost painfully loud even to Blade. The soldiers ignored it, bustling around with the furious purposefulness of ants. A thousand riders mounted up and trotted out to support the morning guard. Another column marched off to protect the siege towers. Other detachments went off to guard the camp and the slaves. All the rest formed into a massive column and marched out of the camp toward Sela's army.

By that time Sela had formed her army for battle, with two lines of androids in front and a third line of humans. A small reserve of androids stood behind the humans. It was a simple formation, as Blade had intended. His total plan for today's battle was complex, but each individual piece of it was fairly simple. It had to be that way—no one under his command was really a trained soldier. If the Shoba's men had come two years later— But they hadn't.

Now the Shoba's army was nearly all out of the camp and forming up for battle. With their gleaming armor and bristling weapons, the Shoba's men looked far more warlike and ferocious than Mak'loh's army with its coveralls and rifles. They formed a line stretching two miles from end to end, and they moved forward with drums, trumpets, and the steady thud of more than thirty thousand pairs of marching feet. The archers led this time, with the musketeers behind. On the flanks rode the cavalry, their massed drums looking like great patches of some weird fungus creeping across the earth. In the gaps between the massed infantry, the cannon rolled forward.

Blade was impressed. It was easy to say that the Shoba's army was formidable. It was another thing to see it going into action and realize just how formidable it was, how much

171

work had gone into creating that discipline and those well-chosen formations.

Blade hoped Sela's army would not crumble away at the mere sight of the enemy's advance. The androids would probably not retreat without human orders, but if panic swept the humans. . . .

Now the Shoba's army was within mortar range of the city. They were coming straight down to the attack, as Blade had hoped. He shifted his gaze to the camp. Soldiers were still moving about inside the palisade, but only a comparative handful. Three or four thousand, at most—not enough to defend the camp against any serious attack, if the palisade were breached.

Silver-gray smoke suddenly gushed up behind Sela's army, swiftly forming into a wall. Blade shrugged. That wasn't quite according to plan. Apparently Sela had decided her people could no longer simply stand and watch the enemy come at them. They had to do something. So she'd ordered the smokescreen laid down. A little ahead of time, to be sure. But of all the things she could have done, it was the one least likely to alarm the enemy.

In fact, it didn't seem to be alarming the enemy at all. The cavalry was reining in, but it didn't matter whether it charged or not. The infantry was marching steadily on, and now the range was down to no more than five hundred yards. They would be within easy range for the mortars inside the walls of Mak'loh.

Sela saw the enemy's cannon pulling to a stop and their crews scurrying about to load and aim them. She felt a cold fluttering in her stomach at the thought of those balls of solid iron smashing into her people. She hoped she'd done enough to steady them, by ordering the smokescreen laid down.

Brrrooooommm. A long, ragged explosion, as half a dozen of the cannon went off together. A ripping sound overhead, like an enormous piece of fabric tearing apart. Then thuds and screams as the balls struck. They'd landed among the reserve androids to the rear. A shiver went along all three lines. Sela tried to will every set of feet in her army to stay rooted to the ground.

The advancing enemy was slowing down. The archers took two extra steps as the musketeers behind them stopped. Then they nocked arrows, drew, and let fly.

Ten thousand arrows whistled down on Sela's army. She heard screams of both fear and pain as they struck, but not many. Every human and android wore a helmet and new armor that protected not only the body but the limbs. Ten thousand arrows that should have cut down half the army killed and wounded less than a hundred.

Without raising her head, Sela lifted her radio to her lips and spoke quickly. "They've opened fire, Geetro. Time for the mortars."

"Understood, Sela." A faint chuckle, then silence.

A second volley of arrows whistled down, and a third. Then there was a long pause. The Shoba's archers seemed to have trouble understanding why the enemy was still on its feet after so many arrows pumped into the ranks. They began to shoot individually at picked targets, rather than in massed volleys.

Before they could shoot many more arrows, the first mortar salvo arrived. Twelve short savage whistles were followed by twelve thunderous explosions. Twelve columns of smoke mushroomed up, carrying with them weapons, bits of armor, chunks of flesh. Around the base of each column was a wide circle where mangled soldiers lay or crawled blindly, as if a giant hand had crushed them flat. The explosions died away. There was a moment of silence, broken only by the screams of the wounded and the whistles as a few hardy archers let fly. Then the second mortar salvo came down, the shells falling almost where the first twelve had. Again the smoke and the flying pieces of what had been human beings; again the ear-pounding roars, again the screams.

Sela raised her rifle and fired twice into the air. On either side of her, human and androids dashed forward. A few went down to lucky arrows. More started to go down as the archers realized they were facing a charge and began shooting flat instead of lofting their arrows, hitting unprotected faces. Musketeers swarmed forward and opened fire. White smoke spread along the enemy's front, joining the gray smoke of the mortar bursts. The cannon kept shooting, and some of their balls plowed into Sela's advancing lines.

None of it did any good. A hundred and fifty yards from the enemy more than eight thousand humans and androids of Mak'loh threw themselves flat on the ground. They raised their rifles and their grenade launchers, and suddenly the air between them and the enemy seemed to turn into white fire.

Now it was as if the great hand had slapped every soldier in the Shoba's front rank in the face. They went down by the hundreds, lying still or kicking furiously, eyes staring, faces bleeding or blackened, smoking patches on chest or stomach or thigh. The riflemen didn't try to aim; they simply pointed their weapons and held down the triggers.

A rapid *pop-pop-pop* sounded as powder exploded in muskets or in musketeer's pouches. A louder series of explosions crashed out, as the grenades started falling around the cannon. The men were suddenly bloody rags, the cannon sagged as wheels were smashed, and barrels of gunpowder ready for loading went off with terrifying roars. On top of it all, the mortar shells still came down, the salvoes growing ragged as some crews fired faster than others.

Now the commaders must have started giving orders, because the Shoba's men began to move back. It was an orderly retreat by men who hadn't lost their courage or forgotten their skills, in spite of the sudden horrors all around them. Both musketeers and archers kept their faces to the enemy and kept firing. They didn't hit very often. Sela's people stayed flat on the ground as they fired. A rifle had the edge over a bow or a musket that way. A man did not have to stand to use it or even load it.

They left bodies behind every step of the way, but eventually the Shoba's men drew out of rifle range. Sela kept her people from leaping up and dashing in pursuit. That would bring them under the mortars, and Blade had many horrible tales of what happened to soldiers who ran in under their own artillery. Sela thought that seeing what the mortars did would be enough. There were broad patches of ground completely carpeted with bodies, not one of them intact, and sodden with blood and pulped flesh.

As if her thought of him had conjured him up, Blade's voice sounded on the radio.

"Sela, hold your position. We're moving out against the camp now. Geetro, it's time for the mobile column to go to work. Are they ready?"

She heard Geetro's voice saying, "Yes," quietly, then heard him shout:

"Mobile column—mount up and move out!"

Blade scrambled down the tree as if it were catching fire, the High Chief's collar bumping and bruising him with every movement. He'd seen the mortars and Sela's people do their work on the Shoba's army. Now it was the turn of the second wave—the mobile column of trucks carrying riflemen and the mortars, and the Warlanders attacking the great camp.

On the lowest branch of the tree, Blade stopped, unslung his rifle, and fired it three times. He heard shouts and more rifle fire from behind him and hoped none of the villagers had hit any of their comrades in their enthusiasm. Then he scrambled down the last twenty feet of the tree and ran forward. Behind him the forest came alive with the crackling branches and scurrying feet as the Warlanders stormed forward.

They came out of the forest and onto the open ground that stretched a mile and a half to the camp. Now they could run even faster. They splashed through a shallow stream as if it weren't there, except for some athletes who leaped it at a single bound. Some of the men fell, others staggered along with twisted ankles, many began to sweat and pant. None of them slowed down as long as they could put one foot in front of the other.

Blade was out ahead of all of them. The camp grew steadily larger ahead. White smoke dotted the top of the palisade as musketeers on guard let fly. The range was impossibly long, but the sight of twelve thousand men running toward them was enough to unnerve even soldiers of the Shoba.

They might be unnerved in the camp, but they could still hold it if the palisade were unbroken. The mortars were supposed to break it open, but where the devil were they? Blade had an unpleasant moment of wondering if the villagers were

175

going to be caught out with an intact palisade. They could be cut to pieces if that happened.

He tried to signal the men behind him to slow down, but they were all too blind with fatigue or excitement or both to pay any attention. The charge swept on toward the camp, and Blade knew that all he could do was lead it and hope.

Sela ran along the lines of her army. Both humans and androids were already at work binding up minor wounds and laying out the dead. Nobody seemed to be ready to lie down unless they were dying or crippled. The courage she saw raised her spirits, while the amount of blood she saw soaking into the ground made her mouth tighten into a grim line.

She reached the far right flank of her army as the mobile column roared out of the smoke behind her.

There were more than a hundred trucks in the column. Ten carried mortars and their crews and ammunition. The rest were packed with android riflemen and humans with grenade throwers. Their sides were built up chest-high with heavy plastic that would stop an arrow or a musket ball. In front each carried a ten-foot metal bar, curved like a bow and studded with foot-long spikes.

On the open ground that the Shoba's men themselves had cleared of all trees and bushes, the trucks could move at nearly their full speed. They poured out of the smoke in a wild uproar of whining, growling engines, rumbling wheels, humans and androids shouting or cursing. None of the riders fired. They had strict orders not to. They only hung on grimly as the trucks swung in a great circle toward the flank of the Shoba's army.

As the trucks came on, trumpets called to the cavalry. A thousand lances dipped, and the hooves of a thousand druns made even more noise than the mobile column. The mortar carriers at the rear of the column slowed down and turned off toward the camp. The others rolled straight on toward the oncoming cavalry.

The Shoba's cavalry and Mak'loh's mobile column closed. Arrows plunged into the solid masses of bodies in the backs of the trucks. Humans and androids tumbled out, to writhe or be crushed flat under the wheels of another truck. Rifles flared and grenades arched out, to pick riders out of their saddles or blow druns limb from limb.

Flesh and blood crashed into metal. Sela put her hands over her ears and closed her eyes. Her mind was simply not made to see and hear what was happening to the Shoba's cavalry, not without breaking. After a little while, though, she forced herself to open her eyes.

She saw druns and their riders going down and trucks crushing them into pulp. She saw other druns impaled on the spikes the trucks thrust in front of them and carried along screaming and writhing. She saw a lance drive through the bubble cab of one truck and skewer the driver. She saw a truck hit a pile of fallen bodies at full speed and flip high into the air, turning end over end and spilling out all its riders. She saw dismounted cavalrymen and dismounted androids rolling over and over, kicking and writhing, like some weird animal with four arms and four legs. She saw five hundred of the Shoba's cavalry die, and the other five hundred break and flee. A shiver went through the infantry when they saw that, and Sela felt like cheering. There *were* things that could shake the solid courage of the Shoba's men.

Then she saw the mortar trucks stopping and the crews leaping out, pulling their clumsy weapons with them and setting them up. She saw the smoke puffs as the mortars opened fire, and finally she saw the familiar smoke columns begin to rise around the camp.

Were the mortars in time to keep Blade from having to throw his mob of villagers against the camp's unbroken defenses? She knew that if that happened, he would die with them. He was that sort of man. If he had been a man of Mak'loh, not of England. . . . Ah well, Geetro was not to be despised.

Blade was fifty yards out in front of his men and less than a hundred yards from the ditch around the fort. Then the first mortar shells struck. They fell inside the camp. He saw the flying bodies and heard the screams. Good shooting, but not good enough. They had to break the palisade, the eight-foot wall of spike-pointed logs, and they had to break it soon.

The mortar shells started coming down faster now. Blade

was almost up to the ditch before the first one struck near the palisade. The logs were cut from full-sized trees, and they would resist anything except a direct hit. Blade hurled himself across the ditch, clawed at the far bank, struggled to hold on to his rifle, and finally pulled himself up onto the level ground. Arrows and musket balls started biting into the earth around him as he stood up and ran on toward the palisade. It loomed higher with every step he took.

Behind him the Warlanders were coming up to the ditch. Some carried ladders or rough planks they threw down and crossed the ditch on those. Others carried bundles of brushwood on their backs and threw those into the ditch until it was filled. A few bold spirits tried to leap across, imitating Blade. Most of those fell into the ditch and floundered about in the mud of the bottom, screaming and swearing. Their comrades dashed up to the palisade on Blade's heels.

The logs were still unbroken when Blade reached them, but for only a moment more after that. A mortar shell came down squarely on top of a cluster of archers on the raised firing platform. The palisade opened like a mouth, spewing flame, smoke, mangled bodies, and chunks of logs. It spewed its mouthful into the faces of the Warlanders, and some of them went down. Others stopped and hung back. Blade saw the danger of the whole attack faltering at the exact moment when it might succeed. He ran toward the gap in the palisade, ignoring the fragments from other mortar bursts whistling about his ears. He found time to shout into his radio:

"Geetro, we're at the camp. Stop those damned mortars—now!"

He got no answer. Then he ran up to the gap and plunged through it, just as another mortar shell burst among the enemy soldiers gathering to defend it. Blade threw himself on his face, and only the blast touched him. The soldiers ready to cut him down took all the fragments. Blade rose to his feet, not quite steady and bleeding from the nose. He took a slow step forward, raised his rifle, saw more enemy soldiers running up to block his path, and charged.

He charged with his rifle wide open, firing from the hip. A dozen men went down before the power cell burned out. Blade snatched it clear, ignoring scorched fingers, but didn't have time to reload. The enemy were all around him. He fought with rifle-butt and bayonet, stabbing throats and cracking skulls, until a sword hacked through the barrel of the rifle. He drew the sword at his belt and hacked a large, clear circle around him. In the process he left an equally large circle of bodies on the ground at his feet.

Then his lone fight was over. The mortar shells stopped falling, and the Warlanders poured in through the gap behind him. They fired their rifles with more enthusiasm than accuracy, shot arrows, swung swords and axes. They nearly trampled Blade into the ground in their desire to come to grips with the Shoba's men.

Blade saw Naran pass, carried on the shoulders of two strong men. The chief carried a rifle and fired as he rode. Each of his bearers carried a spear, and, as they passed enemy corpses, thrust deeply into them to make sure they would stay dead. Then half a dozen men were lifting Blade, and on their shoulders he rode forward after Naran, to the taking of the camp.

The Shoba's men in the camp fought well. For every two of them who died, a Warlands villager also went down. But there were three times as many attackers as there were defenders, so as savage as it was, the battle for the camp did not last long. In half an hour Blade was able to stand beside Naran on top of one of the captured siege towers and watch the last stage of the battle of Mak'loh.

Sela and Geetro joined, and their combined forces moved against the Shoba's army. The riflemen and grenadiers fired from the trucks and from the ground. Overhead the mortars hurled their shells into the enemy's ranks. The Shoba's army gave ground, slowly at first, then not so slowly. They held together longer than any army Blade had ever seen would have done against such an attack.

In the end, though, they gave way. They left the field in good order, but they left it very nearly at a run. They left behind their camp, all their supplies and guns, and nearly half their comrades. The mobile column chased them out of sight, to make sure they went on retreating and didn't try a surprise assault on the city walls somewhere else. Along with the trucks went the last few Watchers, fighting their last battle.

At first Blade was disappointed. He liked the kind of thorough victory that left not one enemy soldier alive and free. Then he realized that perhaps things could be worse. True, if the Shoba got half his army back, he might launch another attack. Let him. With the menace of the Shoba still hanging over them, Mak'loh and the villagers would be forced to stand together.

They had an uneasy alliance. Without a common enemy, it might break up over any one of a dozen issues, starting with the division of the loot from the camp. With an enemy still to face, the alliance might last for many years, until each people could stand on its own. By then, perhaps, each people would also have developed some trust and regard for the other.

So perhaps it was better that some of the Shoba's men were getting away. Mak'loh and the Warlanders might not see how much they needed each other unless somebody forced them. He himself would not be around long enough to do the job; that was certain.

Sela and Geetro didn't enter the camp until the day was fading into twilight. By that time Blade had things sorted out as well as possible. Slaves and prisoners had been counted, guards set, and everyone fed. He greeted Sela and Geetro sitting on the ground, leaning against the nearest backrest. That happened to be the head of a sniffer sprawled on its side. Dead or merely stunned? Blade didn't know and didn't care. He did know that he hadn't slept for nearly two days, and he'd been operating at nearly top speed for several weeks before that. He was not precisely getting old, but he was no longer fresh out of Oxford either.

"Hail, Blade," said Geetro, with an elaborate bow. Sela joined him, although she burst out laughing as she straightened up. After a moment, so did Geetro.

"So—it is done," Sela said. "Blade, do we need to waste breath thanking you?"

It was Blade's turn to laugh. "Not at all," he said. Then, more grimly, he said, "There are many dead and wounded tonight in Mak'loh, who will not be thanking me at all."

"True," said Geetro. "But which is better—some dead

now, or all dead in another hundred years? When those are the only choices, I think even those who have died would wonder. Those who live are sure. Blade, Mak'loh owes you whatever chance it has for a future. May we have the wisdom to make good use of the chance you have given us."

"I share that hope," said Sela. "But what about the villagers of the Warlands? I think it may not be so easy to keep their friendship and get them to work with us."

Blade smiled. Sensible, clear-sighted Sela, keeping her mind on the practical matters and letting Geetro make the grand gestures and use the high-flown words.

"I don't think the villagers will be any problem, as long as there is danger of the Shoba attacking. I would suggest that you deal with Naran as much as possible, for as long as he lives. Don't assume he's got more power than he has though. He always has to take the advice of the other chiefs, and sometimes—sometimes—" Blade put a hand to his temple, as his head whirled in a spasm of dizziness.

"Blade, were you wounded?" asked Geetro. "I should. . . ."

"No," said Blade. "I wasn't wounded. I think. . . ."

Then he could no longer speak, because his head was suddenly a roaring whirlpool of pain that swirled faster and faster. It sucked him in, although he fought to hold onto the world around him. He saw Geetro and Sela leap forward to grip him, but he felt nothing. They felt nothing either—he saw that clearly on their faces. He was as intangible to them as the air. He felt the rifle slung across his chest, he felt the great collar of golden bars around his neck, he *thought* he felt the rough hide of the sniffer's head under his hand.

Then he no longer thought or felt, as the whirlpool of pain sucked him down, out of everything into nothing.

Chapter 22

Lights in a thousand colors and combinations of colors began to swirl around the chair in the glass booth. They formed ghost shapes in one moment and broke apart into a dancing fog in the next. Slowly the lights began to draw together into two coherent shapes.

Richard Blade was coming home, and he was bringing something large with him. *What would it be?* J wondered. At least Blade didn't seem to be on top of it, so it probably wasn't a horse. J remembered vividly the pandemonium the Golden Steed caused when Blade returned with it.

Then the two shapes suddenly took solid form. Blade was sitting in the chair, wearing a stained black coverall, boots, and helmet. A strange-looking rifle was slung across his chest. He looked like a commando back from a difficult mission—except for the massive collar of gold bars hanging around his neck.

Beside the chair Blade's companion took shape. It was not a horse, although it wasn't much smaller. J saw a forest of legs underneath, a forest of spines on top, a long tail waving ominously, great yellow eyes that flared open, a mouth gaping to show rows of white chisel-teeth.

Then the beast was rising on all its feet and coming across the room. J fought down impulses to draw a pistol he wasn't carrying and to jump up on the spectator seat like an old lady who's seen a mouse. He stood motionless as the beast slipped past him and walked up to Lord Leighton. Its nose was twitching furiously, like a rabbit's. The scientist also froze, but J noticed that one hand was only inches from the ALARM button.

Then the beast reared up, the front seven or eight pairs of legs off the ground. It put two pairs of legs on Leighton's shoulders. A long blue tongue crept out between the teeth, and with mightly slurping noises the beast began to wash Leighton's face, like a cat washing one of its kittens. It alternately whimpered with delight and purred with utter contentment as it worked on Leighton.

The scientist didn't move. He didn't dare. J didn't move, and neither did Blade as his awareness of Home Dimension returned. Both J and Blade were struggling too hard not to burst out laughing.

J and Blade were sitting in chairs in Leighton's private office, facing his desk. The desk had been moved eight feet to one side of its original position, to allow room for the sniffer to curl up beside it.

Absently Leighton reached down and scratched the sniffer's head. Its tail (from which the poisoned spines had been carefully extracted) began to wag like a cocker spaniel's, and it began to purr. It purred so loudly that it was like having an outboard motor in the room. All three men had to raise their voices in order to make themselves heard.

"This was quite a successful affair," said Leighton, folding his hands on his desk. "That shock rifle alone is worth a good deal."

"It's a bit short on range for military work in the field," put in J.

"I agree, although with a larger power source the range can undoubtedly be increased. But I was thinking of it more as a police and riot-control weapon. You know the demand for that sort of gear, and you know how hard it is to get something that's genuinely nonlethal. On low power those rifles could break up a riot in minutes without giving anyone anything worse than a headache."

Blade nodded. If the shock rifles could be duplicated, a good many people would gladly pay the Project large sums for the right to manufacture them. That was a big "if," of course—it always had been, with the Project, and it always would be. Fortunately, it had also never been Blade's worry and never would be.

"There's really only one point where I wish we'd had better luck with this mission," Leighton continued. "I really wish Richard had been able to bring back one of the Inward Eye tapes. A machine would have been even better—."

"But hardly possible," put in J.

Leighton frowned at the interruption. "Precisely what I was about to say. Even a tape, though, would have been a good starting point toward duplicating the Inward Eye process. Ah, well, there's no helping it now."

Fortunately, Blade added mentally. He wasn't quite as happy with the mission as Leighton seemed to be. He'd taken gambles that hadn't turned into disasters as much by good luck as by anything he'd done. Not gambles with his own life, but gambles with other people's lives. He'd gambled the lives of everyone in Mak'loh in crippling the city's defenses and starting a civil war. He'd done this on the assumption that the Shoba's army wouldn't strike until the city was ready to defend itself. He'd been right—by the narrowest of margins. But he'd made his assumption on much too little hard evidence. He'd made a mistake.

Was he getting stale or tired? That was a question he'd have to face in the privacy of his own mind, before he even raised it with J. There was no need to breathe a word about it here.

He was certain of one thing though. It wasn't bad luck that he hadn't brought back the secret of the Inward Eye. It was the best sort of luck, for him, for the Project, for Britain, and for the whole world of Home Dimension.

He'd seen too clearly what the Inward Eye could do to people frightened of reality—and there were plenty of people in Home Dimension filled with that same fear. Too many of them had already retreated into drink, drugs, mystical religions—a dozen strange ways of life. None of these cut them off from the world and sucked them in as thoroughly as the Inward Eye. None of these was so dangerous.

To be sure, Home Dimension might in time develop something like the Inward Eye on its own. Blade couldn't do anything about that. But in the meantime, he could be happy that he hadn't brought back from the city of the living dead a secret that could bring his own world down in ruins.